**He was the same man she'd seen outside her home last night, and now he'd walked into her store with enough weapons to start another world war!**

It was a glamour, a spell to help people see only what they wanted to see when they looked at him. Theo narrowed her eyes, looking *under* the shield of magick, and saw that he was wearing knives strapped to his body, and a pair of bright silver guns. And to top off the utter impossibility, he had the leather-wrapped hilt of a *sword* poking up over his left shoulder.

*What, he just couldn't find anything else to wear this morning?* she thought, and found herself backing up.

Theo took two more startled steps back, her left hip hitting the glass cabinet that held the cash register. She barely noticed the flare of pain that caused. "What *are* you?" she asked, and saw something—a blush—rising up his clean-shaven cheeks. Blushing. A man who knew her name came strolling into her shop wearing guns, and he was *blushing*?

"You might not believe me," he said, and pulled something that looked like a business card out of his pocket. He offered it to her, still not looking up at her face. "I have several things to tell you, and I just…" He trailed off.

Theo couldn't back up any more. The glass cabinet was behind her. The air in the store stirred uneasily, the wards sensing her fear. How had he gotten through them, armed like that? "What are you?" she asked again. "Was that you, following me last night?"

He was still offering her the card. "All I can tell you right now…" He broke off and glanced at Suzanne. Theo looked back at Elise, who was leaning on a bookcase, grinning. "…is that you're in danger, and I'm here to help."

To Nicholas D., as ever and always.


Coming in 2005 from Lilith Saintcrow

Storm Watcher
Fire Watcher
Cloud Watcher

# Dark Watcher

**\*\*\***

# Lilith Saintcrow

ImaJinn
Books

Dark Watcher
Published by ImaJinn Books

ISBN: 0-9759653-2-8

10 9 8 7 6 5 4 3 2 1

PUBLISHER'S NOTE:
This book is a work of fiction. Names, characters, places and incidents are products of the author's imagination or are used fictitiously. Any resemblance to actual events or locales or persons, living or dead, is entirely coincidental.

Books are available at quantity discounts when used to promote products or services. For information please write to: Marketing Division, ImaJinn Books, P.O. Box 545, Canon City, CO 81215-0545, or call toll free 1-877-625-3592.

Cover design by Patricia Lazarus

**ImaJinn Books**
P.O. Box 545, Canon City, CO 81215-0545
Toll Free: 1-877-625-3592
http://www.imajinnbooks.com

# One

The rain poured down, glittering and flashing, smashing its silver needles against the pavement and the blank buildings. Theodora locked the shop's front door and flattened her hand on the cold glass. Her rings sparkled, and the flash of her triggering the wards was almost hidden.

Then again, nobody without Power would see it anyway. And nobody *with* Power would be out on a night like tonight. There was the freezing rain, and the persistent smell of danger in the wet, icy air. Theo slipped her gloves on and held her long woolen pea coat closed at her throat. Her scarf was wrapped around her neck, and her grandmother's ruby necklace was a comforting weight against her breastbone.

Theo yawned and started her walk home. *Maybe I should stop and get some tea,* she thought, and then smiled at herself. *You're just hoping to find someone to talk to, Theo. Admit it.*

Business had been good lately, but very little of it had been serious. Some high-school kids had discovered the Craft, and since most of them were upper-middle-class, they had to have all the toys. Well, that was good for Theo's wallet. Good for a trip to Mexico, to lay in the sun and turn brown and listen to the voices in the sand and the sea. Zihuatanejo, rhymed with tomato, and she was saving for that vacation.

There were the regulars, too, and her employees—Mari was busy getting ready for her finals, and Elise had something special in mind that she'd been stocking pink quartz and rose-oil for. *Another bring-me-love spell. I wonder for who? Maybe Mark, he's been moping around lately. Poor man. If Elise would only look his way for a moment, she might find more than she bargains for. But then again, he's too much of a nice guy for her. She likes bad boys…*

Theo put her head down and walked briskly up the dark street, her long chestnut hair already damp. It would be sodden by the time she reached the Creation.

She took one quick glance back when she reached the end

of the street. Her shop—the Magick Cauldron—lay dark and glittering faintly in its brick building. The wards were glimmering to her Sight, and all was as it should be.

Theo sighed. She loved the shop, and she loved her life, but…sometimes she wished…

It was normal to wish, but a witch had to be careful of her wishes. "A little excitement," she said, softly. "And maybe…Goddess, would it be too much to ask to find a decent guy? I mean, the last time I dated was two whole years ago, and that was such a disaster. Then again, I did it to myself, by wishing for a man and not being careful about the terms and conditions."

Theo laughed. There was nobody on the street, so she wouldn't look too crazy, walking along and talking to herself. The wind was uneasy tonight, whispering between the buildings, but Theo simply walked a little faster, the rain wetting her hair and her face, soaking into her coat. Danger in the air? Let it come. Theo was safe enough in the hands of the Goddess.

She began to hum. Suzanne had written another song, and it was hard to get it out of her head. *Bring me down to the god in the glen, bring me down to the green trees dancing—*

Well, what would it hurt? Theo lifted her voice, singing. Her voice would be lost in the wind and the rain. "Bring me down to the god in the glen, bring me down to the green trees dancing. Bring me down to the Lady's mirror, bring me down to the place of the dance…da-da-da-dum, bring me a song, da-da-da-dum, bring me a stone, da-da-da-dum, bring me along, along to the place of the Lady's throne—"

She had a pleasant contralto, and the wind answered, sliding between the buildings and suddenly smelling more like spring than the end of fall, just before Samhain. The trees, losing their leaves, rattled in the sudden wind, adding their voices to hers. The rain felt sweet for a moment, and warm, and Theo's laughter echoed in the concrete canyons of the city.

# Two

"That's her?" Dante asked. "That's the target?" He couldn't keep the disbelief out of his voice.

"It is." Hanson crouched out of sight, looking dark and miserable in the rain. They were on the roof of a bank, watching the woman. "According to the intel, that's the next one. They think she's the most dangerous to them. They could be right, you know."

Dante stuffed his hands in his coat pockets and looked down again. His senses were sharper than any normal's, and he could see the glimmer in the air around the woman. She was tall and slim and moving as if she was dancing down the dark rain-slick sidewalk. The power trailing her smelled like green growing things, and she was making enough noise to be heard throughout the entire city. "They could be," he agreed. "She's lit up like a marquee sign. How do *they* find them?" he asked, shaking his head. The rain was slicking his short black hair to his forehead, and he was beginning to feel the cold. He ignored it. There was so much to ignore in this line of work. "Don't they care that the Lightbringers..." He trailed off. He asked the question often, and nobody seemed to have a good answer.

"Who knows? They're on a Crusade, man. They don't care. Got their own brave new world to bring." Hanson blinked, and then looked around again. "I've got to go, I've got my own witch to look after. You got the dossier?" He knew very well that Dante had the slim file and would memorize and destroy it in the next twelve hours.

"Of course I got it, quit bugging me. I can do this." Dante looked back down to where the woman had stopped and was looking in a shop window. The Darkness inside him shifted uneasily, and he forced it down, ignoring the fresh bite of pain. To be this close to a Lightbringer made it more active. "So what does she do?"

"Runs that little occult shop. You can see the shields from

here, man. She's like a volcano. You'd better go." Hanson shifted from foot to foot and grinned. It was a wolf's lazy grin. His blue eyes glittered in the uncertain light—his blond hair was much darker now, slick with rain. "They're close. Whole damn city crawling with them."

"All right, go back to watching your witch, and I'll go and watch mine. Call if you need me." Dante made the offer, knowing it would prick Hanson's pride.

"I don't need you. I've been doing just fine at this for a long time."

"Not long enough, if you're still doing it." Dante gathered himself and leapt lightly to the top of the brick wall. He looked down at the concrete four stories below. His coat moved around his legs—a long black leather trench coat, which went really well with the whole punk-angel fashion trip—and he glanced back at Hanson. "Honor, brother."

"Duty, brother. Good luck."

Dante nodded and leapt.

There was a breathless moment of almost-flight, the laws of physics bending just a little, and then his boots touched down. He drew the rainy air around him like a cloak and followed the trail the woman had left in the air.

If the Crusade was in this city, they were going to move on her soon. It was only a matter of time. *A witch running an occult shop,* he thought. *Gods. They have no sense of discretion anymore. Can't blame them, though. Lightbringers.*

Dante lengthened his stride a little and hurried after the witch.

# Three

The Creation was decorated for Halloween, a huge orange paper pumpkin hanging from the ceiling and orange pumpkin lights strung in the picture window. It had been a hippie co-op in the seventies, and abandoned after the co-op folded. Abe Francklin had bought it, and had turned it into a coffeehouse right before coffee had become a gourmet experience. The floor was concrete, and a few straggling green plants perked almost visibly as soon as Theo closed the door and shook her long hair out. The tables were topped with marble—Abe had bought them from a short-lived ice cream parlor in the very first days of urban renewal. They always seemed about to tip, just like the rocking wooden benches. The walls were covered with a violent jungle mural that some local artist had painted in an alcoholic haze. Theo liked it; it was green, and it had trees.

It was a Wednesday night and not very busy. Joffrey coughed in the corner, but Todd was nowhere to be seen, probably working late. Vail waved in greeting. There were a few other people, none of them regulars. Theo slipped her coat and gloves off, and Sage cursed from behind the barista's counter. He'd taken over from Matt Delgado, after Delgado had quit last spring and opened up the Free Shelter. There was a mystery there, but one that Theo was comfortable not knowing. It had to do with last winter, and that had been a hard one. She'd lost several patients that winter, to the cold and to…other things. "Good evening to you too, Sage," she said, and wrinkled her nose as a drift of cigarette smoke slid by. "What's wrong?"

Sage, a thin, tall, red-haired man working towards a law degree, peered out from behind the red hulk of the espresso machine. "What the… Oh, hi, Theo. Damn machine—" His eyes were wide and dark, and he had faint lines scored between his coppery eyebrows. He had a long nose, long fingers, and a gold earring in his left ear. His hair was stiff with gel and spiked to within an inch of its life.

"What's wrong with it?" Theo asked, dropping her coat and her gloves on the table by the door. She hadn't carried a purse today, knowing that it would likely rain. "Let me take a look."

"You're a lifesaver, Theo. How's business over at Ye Olde Witch Shoppe?" Sage wiped his hands on a rag and poured a white china mug full of coffee.

Theo came around the edge of the counter and examined the machine. "Oh, my," she said. "Can you bring me some towels? I think this will get messy. Business is fine, and I don't think I'm renaming the shop anytime soon, thank you. Get me a screwdriver, too."

"As you command, oh princess," he said, and winked one brown eye. Theo laughed and pushed her hair back over her shoulder.

"Get going. Honestly, I don't know why Abe doesn't buy a new machine." she started working on the stuck filter, and burned her finger on it. It was still hot. "Ow!"

"He's cheap, that's why. Hurt yourself?" Sage looked contrite. "God, Theo, I'm sorry."

"Don't worry about it. Just a little burn…" Theo took a towel, wrapped it around the handle and then around the cup of the espresso-box. "Stand back, ladies and gentlemen, I'm about to perform some magic. Get me that screwdriver, will you?"

"Oh, yeah. Sure." Sage set off for the tiny room where they kept the tools and the stereo system, and Theo leaned close to the coffee machine.

"You want to work for me," she said, quietly. "It's all right, I know you're tired. Just a little, now." She used the same tone that she would on a frightened beast, and she was rewarded with a pop and a puff of steam. Thankfully, the towel caught the steam and the coffee grounds, and she wiped up and tossed the towel in the "dirty" box. "There we are," she said, softly. "Thank you." She sketched a quick rune on the backsplash of the machine—Tiw, for the god of justice and blacksmiths. Machines were his purview. She thought for a moment, and then added the Vulca symbol. The machine needed all the help it could get.

Her fingers throbbed. *That'll teach me to grab without looking,* she thought, and hummed a snatch of the melody again. The pain faded, and she shook it out through the tip of her finger, careful not to flick it towards any glass. The concrete floor groaned, accepting the pain, and then subsided.

"Your screwdriver, Your Witchiness," Sage said, presenting her with a red-handled Phillips head. "Will that work?"

"It'll work just fine. How about pouring me a cup of tea, since I'm fixing your machine?" She deftly popped out the offending part, and took a look. There. A coffee bean, stuck in the machine. "Now how did that get there? Don't tell me, it just got up and leapt in there."

"I don't know," Sage said, rinsing out a small white teapot with hot water to warm it. "What kind of tea? The peppermint again?"

"No, some chamomile. I think I need the calming, I feel a little wild tonight. What's happening on the Ave?" Theo popped the part back on, tightened the screws, and then checked the rest of the machine. It should hold up for another few days.

"Oh, you know, everyone's nervous. Wonder what the gang boys are doing for Halloween." He poured the hot water in and added the tea bag. "Sounds like they have a big party planned. You want something to eat?"

"Do you have any of Charlene's pumpkin loaf? I'll take a slice of that." Theo finished, and she mopped up the water that had spread on the counter and the stray coffee grounds. She took a deep breath and glanced out the front window. Nothing there but the night, drenched in freezing rain. Why did she feel so nervous?

"Okay, pumpkin loaf it is. Joe Cool's getting kind of nutty. You know he started saying the other night that there're werewolves in the city?" Sage laughed, his quick fingers moving deftly. "How crazy is that?"

"Very," Theo murmured. Actually, it wasn't crazy at all. She knew some of the Kine in the city. "How did he arrive at this conclusion?"

"He said he saw one down at the wharves. But he's been

drinking again. You know how it is."

Theo nodded. She did indeed know how it was. Her earrings swung back and forth, tapping on her cheeks. They were garnets set in long twisting Celtic spirals made of silver, for luck and protection. She had felt fiery today. Her grandmother's necklace sparked against her neck.

Theo tapped her ringed fingers on the counter, her eyes drawn to the night outside again. The stereo must have clicked over to a new CD, because the Tragic Diamonds started to wail about that no-good Jimmy Jingo, that lowdown dirty beast. It was a song Theo knew by heart.

"The Diamonds," she said. "That's their demo?"

"Oh, yeah." Sage nodded enthusiastically. "Elise brought it by. Good stuff, huh?"

"Fantastic," she said, and accepted the plate with two pieces of pumpkin loaf on it. Suzanne and Elise had written that song together about one of Theo's ex-boyfriends. It had been extremely therapeutic. "Thank you. I'll come back for the tea—"

Sage blinked at her. "Na, I'll carry it. You're sitting next to the door?"

The door opened, the bell hung on it jingling, and Theo heard a familiar whistling voice. "Hey, Sage, wassup?"

"Oh, God." Sage rolled his eyes, and then he turned around. "Hello, Grody. What hole did you crawl out of?"

Theo sighed. She carried her pumpkin loaf around the counter and was confronted with the vision of Grody digging in his pockets for change. "I know I got it," he said, and reeled. His nose was bright red, and the smell of gin exhaled from him in powerful waves. "I got a dollar for coffee, right here."

Theo looked over. Her eyes met Sage's, and Sage's eyebrows rose. Theo put her pumpkin loaf down on the table and fished a five-dollar bill from her coat pocket. Her coat was beginning to steam in the heat. "Here," she said. "I'll buy you a cup of coffee, Grody. Go ahead and sit down." She took the man's elbow.

He was at least six inches taller than her, and his dirty pants were held up with a bit of string. His shoes were canvas, his left big toe was sticking out from a hole, and his jacket stank. Theo did not allow her nose to wrinkle again. He had a round face, even though his neck was skinny, and his gray hair formed a long, matted fringe around his bald head.

Grody looked down at her. "Theo!" he crowed, delighted. "Theo!"

"Shhh, Grody." She hushed him gently, and he quieted. "Now sit down. Sage is anxious tonight, so we've got to help him out."

Grody nodded, his eyes focusing over her shoulder. He had at least three days growth of beard. How had he managed to get gin? Where was Taz? Old, stick-thin Taz usually kept Grody out of trouble. Theo sighed, guided Grody onto the bench across from hers, and made him sit down by tugging on his arm. Then she turned back to the counter. Sage was shaking his head.

She stepped back up to the counter and gave him the five. "A cup of coffee for Grody, and then I'll get him out of here and to the drunk tank. I promise."

Sage just shook his head. "You're a softie, Theo. You're going to get mugged or worse one of these days. You and your strays—"

"I didn't ask for your opinion," Theo said, maybe a little sharply. She had been looking forward to a nice leisurely cup of tea and her pumpkin loaf while she chatted with Sage and watched the usual nightly crowd fill the Creation. And she could have traced out her plans for Mexico in her little notebook. "I don't think it's a crime to have a soft heart, Sage. Not if you're firm when you have to be." She wiped her hand on her hip, pulling at her wine-red sweater. Her skirt was damp at the bottom edge. "Coffee, and my tea, please."

He took her five and handed her four ones in change. "You fixed my machine," he said. "I won't charge you for the tea or the pumpkin loaf. What's Abe going to do, fire me?'

"I certainly hope not. Who would nurse that machine along?" Theo felt her shoulders relaxing, and smiled. When Sage turned to pour Grody's coffee, she put the extra four dollars in his tip jar. Then she carried her teapot and cup over to the table. "He's bringing your coffee, Grody, and then we'll take a walk. It's cold out tonight, isn't it?"

Grody nodded, his greasy, thinning hair swinging forward. "Bad things out tonight. Wolves in the clouds."

Theo felt a cool finger trace its way up her spine. "Really?" she asked lightly. Sage brought the coffee, and Theo lowered herself onto the bench. She picked up a slice of pumpkin loaf and bit into it. "You don't say. Here's your coffee. Thank you, Sage."

Sage grinned at her. "Anything for you, Theo. Thanks for fixing the old beast." He went back behind the counter, whistling along with the Diamonds, and Theo felt another smile tugging at her lips. This time she gave in, and smiled. She pushed her coat down onto the bench next to her and laid her gloves atop it.

"Well, Grody," she said. "Drink your coffee, and then we'll take a walk."

Grody beamed at her, the scars on his forehead white against his flushed skin. Nobody knew what had turned him into what he was—and Theo didn't want to know. She was careful not to touch him, but she did slide her plate over, with the other piece of pumpkin loaf. "Here," she said.

"Thanks, Theo," he said, a little sadly, and sipped at his scalding coffee. He held the steaming cup in his chapped hands, and shivered slightly.

"You're welcome," she said, meaning it, and started to drink her tea.

# Four

Dante was across the street, melted into the bricks and the deeper shadows of the convenient doorway he'd found, when the witch came out. He scanned the street, slowly.

Nothing. Nothing but the witch and a drunk normal. He was leaning on her, and Dante could smell the alcohol on him. Gin, and lots of it. The normal smelled like vomit as well, and the witch's clean scent, mixed with the human stench, was almost nauseating.

Dante's lips peeled back from his teeth. What was this?

He strained his ears through the smacking sound of rain and the now-moaning wind.

"—to a warm bed," she said. Her voice was pleasant, low and husky, and she didn't sound concerned or fearful. As a matter of fact, she sounded calm. Dante's body clenched around the sweet contralto purr of that voice. That had never happened before.

"Won't that be nice?" she said, and the pain twisted in Dante's bones and quieted a little.

"They don't like me there, Theo," the normal said, in a whiny petulant voice. Dante found a silent growl edging its way out of his chest and stopped himself, aghast. What was wrong with him?

The woman stopped and looked around, her long hair moving damply in the sodden wind. He caught a flash of green—her eyes? Her aura? He stopped breathing, folding himself up inside his shielding.

He felt her attention sweep the street, like green flame. Gods, but she was powerful. How had she escaped the Dark before this? Just dumb luck, or had she been sensible enough to keep her head down when it felt dangerous outside?

He strained his eyes. A slice of a cheekbone, a flash of her mouth. Nothing more. He couldn't tell what she looked like. But he could follow the green, earth-smelling aura of power around her. It dyed the air with streaks of dark, brilliant green, like an emerald held up to the sun. And the fringes of the green were always seeking around her, excellent shielding. If he hadn't been tuned to—

She hurried on, her voice a soothing burr, talking to the normal in hushed tones. Dante could still smell the alcohol from here.

He could also smell something else.

He wrapped the rainy darkness around himself and waited silently. Something else was amiss here.

Then he spotted it—an amorphous blot of shadow, following the witch's glow. Something misshapen, ugly.

A Seeker.

Adrenaline jolted through Dante's system, but he savagely clamped his control down. *What is wrong with me?* He had never had any problem with control before. Never in all the time he had been a Watcher had he hesitated even for a moment.

He ghosted down the street after the Seeker. If all went well, tonight would see one dead Seeker, and hopefully a live witch to someday add to Circle Lightfall.

If all went well.

Dante shifted to an effortless lope, a pace that would let him overtake the Seeker before the witch even sensed its presence. He cut through the rainy night, and there was a glint coming from the silver guns in his hands.

# Five

"Not again," Browley said, her eyebrows raised. She hooked her thumbs in her uniform belt. The police blue looked good on her, and her short bomber jacket accentuated her trim figure. "Theodora Morgan, you can't be serious." She was a lean, rawboned woman who looked unfinished, even in her uniform. The homeless children on the Avenue, with rare humor, called her Officer Browbeat. Despite that, she was tough, competent, and sometimes even compassionate. She was known for fairness.

"Oh, just put him in the tank," Theo said. "He'll cause some harm if he's out there alone tonight. Come on, Marla. You know I'm doing the right thing." She was trying not to wheedle.

"Oh, I know. You always do." Browley ran her fingers back through her short dark hair and then shrugged. "All right, I'll see if I can take him in. Hang on." She turned aside, and spoke into her radio. It burbled and squawked. Theo had to be careful not to get too close to it. Her aura could short out electrical appliances sometimes, especially on a night like this.

Theo waited patiently, rain soaking her hair. Grody was all but asleep on his feet, swaying and making little burbling noises. It was the gin, rising to his head. He would pass out soon, and he'd catch pneumonia or worse sleeping on the cold concrete ground.

Theo risked a little bit of magick. Humming softly, she flattened her gloved hand against Grody's jacket sleeve. He smelled awful. He must have vomited on himself before coming into the Creation. She breathed out through her mouth and let the healing pass through her.

It was as if she stood in the middle of a great swelling organ note, resonating in the world around her. Green light flashed, and the smell of a forest—incongruous here in the city—breathed through the rainy air.

"Okay, Theo. I can take him in." Browley sighed and

scratched at her wet forehead. "I swear, you and your strays. When are you going to give it up?" Her eyes were dark with something very much like disgust as she looked at the hiccupping, swaying Grody.

"As soon as nobody needs my help, I'll give it up," Theo replied. Her hair was beginning to drip at the ends, and she only wanted to be home with her feet up and a hot cup of tea. "Thank you, Marla. I owe you one."

"Just whistle me up some luck," Browley said, with a smile. She was not nearly as tough as she wanted to appear. "Okay, Grody, come on. The paddy wagon's gonna meet me a block from here, and you'll sleep on the County's tab tonight."

"Go with Marla, Grody," Theo said softly, reinforcing her words with a small *push*. "Be peaceful. It's all going to be fine." She didn't dare to use even an eighth of her strength in the *push*. It would very likely tip Grody into unconsciousness and give him a screaming headache to boot. Alcohol was tricky when mixed with a *push*. You could never tell how it was going to react.

She watched Marla steer Grody down the street. He went docilely. Theo sighed, snugged her scarf a little closer to her neck, and traced a rune in the air. *Beorc*, the birch tree, for healing and strength. The cop and the drunk both paused, and then they continued on.

She allowed herself to sigh, and turned around. It would take her a good twenty minutes to walk home from here. She had been intending to walk Grody all the way to the precinct house, if she had to. Thank the Lady that wasn't necessary.

Theo walked along, her boots making reassuringly crisp sounds on the pavement. She felt the rain soaking into her ankle-length skirt and grimaced at the thought. It was going to be a very wet—and very *cold*—walk home. *But Mexico. Mexico in three months. White sand beaches, blue water, daiquiris on the patio.*

She began to sing again, thinking that she could use the practice, and she would also be able to keep warmer if she stirred some of the Power around her. "Da-da-da-dum, bring me a song, da-da-da-dum, bring me a stone, da-da-da-dum,

bring me along, along to the place of the Lady's throne—"
She liked the chorus, it was a beautiful melody, and it carried
Power well. She repeated it again, her voice rising, silvery,
like a bird, flashing through the rain. Presently she had changed
the words, and was singing, "Mexico, Acapulco...Tenochtitlan,
white sand, da-da-dum, blue water, da-da-dum...Zihuatanejo,
da-da-dum..."

She did not see the shadow across the street, rising up
through the rain and then swelling with poisonous intent. She
was too busy singing, and presently she started to dance a
little, swaying down the rainy sidewalk. Life was good.

# Six

The woman was blithely tripping down the sidewalk, oblivious to the Darkness gathering around her. Dante cursed to himself. Where had the drunken normal disappeared to? Why had she turned back? Couldn't she *see* the Seeker?

No, of course she couldn't. The Seeker was hiding itself from her, and she was a Lightbringer, so she didn't suspect a thing. It took a bit of the Darkness to really understand and see what the Dark was capable of, and a Lightbringer wouldn't have Darkness in her. That was a Watcher's job, to see the Dark and know it for what it was. Fight fire with fire—and to fight a Seeker, it took a Watcher.

The Seeker swelled, preparing itself. It was blindly waiting for the woman to come within range, and then it would strike like a snake. Seekers were great predators. They had to be. They lived on psychics and also cannibalized other little pieces of Darkness. Only this one might be a created Seeker, since the Crusade was in town. If it was a created Seeker, the Master—a live Knight of the Crusade—had to be around here somewhere. He had to be close to control the Seeker. A created Seeker left to its own devices gradually faded and vanished, and that was expensive, given the hours of ritual required to create or trap one.

Dante's guns vanished. For this, he couldn't use them. To risk alerting the witch to his presence was dangerous at this point, and charging in, bullets blazing, was guaranteed not to give her confidence in his peaceful intentions. Not to mention that a stray bullet might catch her. He didn't want to make any mistakes tonight.

He made himself silent and deadly, slipping through the rain-washed air, his hands now down low and close to his body, two black-bladed knives reversed along his forearms. Knife work—silent and close, he could rip the Seeker loose from its mooring in the physical world, and with any luck, the energies released would backlash onto the Knight. *If* it was a created

Seeker, and *if* he could hit it low and fast enough.

He was almost within range when the woman took the last few dancing steps, waltzing right into the Seeker's strike zone. Dante cursed internally and streaked for the swollen, brooding shadow.

He met it just as it started its strike. It had not achieved its full lethal speed yet. Still, the impact jarred his teeth, but he was moving faster, and he carried it with him into a handy alleyway. Bricks shattered. *Enough noise to wake the dead,* he thought, and schooled himself, bringing in the knives fast and low. The Power he'd charged his fists with sparked venomously scarlet, and he let out a sharp breath as claws made out of pure shadow raked his side. If he believed too much, they could kill him, a psychic wound becoming a physical one.

He brought the knife in his left hand up and then tore down, neatly carving the back of the Seeker open along its barbed spine. Fluid bubbled and smoked. The black rune-chased steel of his knife blade was more damaging to the Seeker than sunlight, and the thing howled inaudibly.

Dante shook the stunning sound out of his head. It was a tearing wail at the very upper reaches of his mental range, and he thanked the gods that the woman was probably gone by now. The Seeker imploded, black light fizzing against the concrete, and Dante found himself on his knees, shaking his head, trying to clear it from both the ringing impact and the Seeker's dying scream. There was no explosion of wasted Power, so it had been a created Seeker. And the energy had backlashed on the Knight—zombie or live—that had leashed it and brought it here. That was going to be one unhappy piece of dead flesh in a few hours. The power would eat it until nothing remained. Not a bad night's work.

Training brought him to his feet, and he quickly scanned the alley. Nothing left but a slight reverberation that would make the alley uncomfortable for any psychic passing by. They would hurry on, not knowing why they felt like getting out of here.

*Good. Clear.* Then he ran silently for the mouth of the

alley.

The woman was standing two blocks down, completely still and silent. Her long dark hair was dripping, and she was listening, her head upflung. She wore a dark skirt that swirled around her ankles, and silver glittered in the one ear that Dante could see.

She waited, standing there, obviously listening.

*Go on.* Dante thought. *You're safe now. Go on home, so I can rest.*

She whirled, facing him, her skirt and hair flaring out, as if she'd heard him.

Dante stopped breathing. His labored heart and starved lungs ached and demanded that he breathe, but he overrode them until she slowly turned back the way she had been walking and continued on. This time she walked quickly, the little green fingers of her shielding waving like sea anemones. He would bet that she was quivering with nervous energy, even though not a whisper of it escaped. Enough shielding to keep her thoughts to herself, but not enough to keep a Seeker from cracking her open and devouring her like a tasty little morsel.

He finally permitted himself to take a deep breath and began to trail silently behind her. *That's right, go home. You're safe, I promise.*

His side was aching It was not bleeding; it was just...aching. If he ignored it, it would go away.

# Seven

The relief Theo felt when she unlocked her own front door was immediate, deep—and a little frightening. She must have imagined that awful chilling scream—as if something was dying. But nothing had died tonight. She hadn't felt the peculiar wrenching that death echoed within her presence. She had only heard that scream and then felt a silence—a silence so large as to be unnatural. And then...*that's right, go home. You're safe, I promise.*

A voice that came out of the air itself. A voice like dark old whiskey. Someone...But it could have just been her imagination.

She slipped inside her front hall and shut the door, locking it securely. Then she slumped, trembling, against the door's familiar comfort. Her cat Thorin raced to the door, meowing, and then skidded to a stop, catching wind of her uneasiness. His fur puffed out from his round black body, and he hissed.

"It's all right, Thorin," she lied to him, and he spat and scrambled away. She heard him run up the stairs. He would run under her bed and crouch there, until she calmed down. He was too sensitive to her.

Her house was dark. She usually enjoyed coming home and turning the lights on, but tonight, for some reason, she rested against the door for perhaps fifteen seconds. Then she walked deliberately down the hall and into the large living room. She walked up to the large picture window looking out over her front garden and the street. A quiet, middle-class street, with slightly weedy lawns and lovely old trees that arched over the narrow sidewalks. Rain was still coming down, not as hard as it had been, but Theo thought perhaps the rain would crest early in the morning. Her weathersense told her so.

She stood in the window and looked out. Here, behind the wards she had laid so carefully and woven into the very fiber of the walls and floors, she could let her own personal wards slip a little. Some of the uneasiness she was feeling leapt free, making the walls groan slightly. The floor under her creaked.

She watched.

After perhaps ten minutes, during which she dripped a large puddle onto her hardwood floor, she tensed.

*There.*

A man walked past her house. He didn't pause and look at her little green two-story house, with its white-painted trim and its window boxes still full of trailing geraniums, or her garden that was still neat and orderly, even under the drift of leaves from last night's storm. She had cut back all her herbs for the winter, and racks of them hung drying in the garage. No, he didn't pause at all, just walked past her house like a shark would circle, with an even pace and a cool disdain. Theo could feel his tension, though, and his attention trained on the house. Watching her. She had felt someone watching her, and now…

That scream. What could it have been? She'd felt danger in the air, but she'd assumed it was simply the general air of nervousness two weeks from Samhain. The Veil was getting thin, the border between this world and the next gradually losing much of its solidity, and people always felt it. She hadn't felt the sharp sense of impending disaster that had always warned her before.

*Yeah, warned me to leave every place I've ever settled. And now…Do I have to leave here too?*

Theo unwrapped her scarf from her neck, watching as the man cruised by. He passed under a streetlight, and she saw black hair, sticking to his head with rain. A long coat, hands stuck in pockets. But he didn't slouch. His posture was almost military-straight, and he moved too gracefully. Almost inhumanly gracefully. Like a shark, gliding through blue water.

She decided to test him a little.

The wards on the house quivered under her will, moving gently like seaweed. She pushed past them, casting her senses out, and reached towards the man who had paused under the street lamp as if looking at it. *Who would be taking a walk in pouring cold rain and stopping to look at street lamps?* she wondered idly, and then felt the hard, cool edge of someone else's warding.

Whoever he was, he was good. Almost nonexistent to even

her sharp senses. Theo was looking, and she almost missed the telltale ripple in the air when he seemed to vanish beneath the street lamp. Rain fell through where he had been standing.

She drew in a sharp breath. Unbidden, the image of a knight rose in her mind. A knight holding a bloody sword and pushing back the visor of his helm, sweat staining a pale face. *That's right, go home. You're safe, I promise.*

Theo shook her head. That was useless. *No flights of fancy,* she reminded herself, sternly. *Here is a mystery. Did a psychic man follow me home? Is he looking for a coven? Are we in danger?*

She thought of walking Grody on the cold street, and she shivered. He could have been hurt. And Marla...

Abruptly, anger rose, and Theo took a deep breath and counted to ten. Another deep breath, another ten slow counts. Then she quickly, decisively, walked to the right side of the window and pulled on the cord that closed the drapes.

"Blue sea," she whispered to herself. "White sand beaches. Suntan and seashells."

She went around the house, pulling drapes and closing blinds, until she had completed the task. Only then did she turn the lights on in the kitchen and the living room and decide to take her wet clothes off. From there it was easy to follow her nightly routine—a shower, a dry silk dress, a cup of tea steaming in her hand as she walked from room to room, checking her altars and the leaves laid on her hearth, her mother's cauldron and the carved-stone pentacle. She touched her athame, her ritual knife, which was laid across the runespell she was working for Moira, to help her through the chemotherapy.

She noticed, finally, that she was cruising aimlessly through the house, and she settled herself on the couch in the living room. Now that she knew someone was watching, it seemed impossible to ignore the faint disturbance at the very edge of her sensing range. It remained there as the cup of tea cooled and grew cold in her hand, and as the heat pump clicked on and warm air soughed through the house. She didn't even try to read, it would have been a disservice to a book to try and read while she was so distracted. Instead, she meditated. Thorin finally crept down from the upstairs and curled in her lap, purring and kneading with his sharp claws to get her attention. She petted him absently, smoothing his black fur and watching as his yellow eyes drift closed with contentment.

*That's right, go home. You're safe, I promise…*That voice. Male, deep and cool. Old whiskey and smoke, that voice. Nothing she had ever heard before…not even in a dream.

Finally, Theo lit some cedar incense and dumped the cold tea out. She went up to bed, carrying Thorin and taking a small purple velvet pillow Suzanne had given her, stuffed with dried lavender and hops, with a moonstone in it. This she tucked under her pillow when she pulled back the covers on her bed. She never bothered to make the bed, just left it in disarray, even after she changed the sheets. Pale linen and a sage-green down comforter, pillows that she usually propped behind her while she finished reading whatever book she had set herself to that day. It was her haven, the place she retreated to.

She turned the lights out and stood, irresolute, by the side of the bed. Thorin had already hopped up and was turning around in a circle on his pillow, the one right next to Theo's. He looked up at her and made a short inquiring sound, asking when she was coming to bed.

Then she walked to the front bedroom, the guest bedroom, and looked down on the street from its vantage point.

Nothing. She could still feel him, but faintly, as if he was sleeping, or concentrating on something else. The vanishing trick he'd done was good, and she wanted to figure out how he'd done it.

*Why is he watching me?*

That was, of course, an excellent question. Theo considered it, and then decided that the answer wasn't likely to come tonight. So she should sleep. As Suzanne often said, if there was to be a funeral in the morning, the living had to be well-rested to plan it.

Theo laid down in her bed, pulled the covers up, and stared into the darkness, hearing her cat purr and waiting for sleep to come.

# Eight

Dante read the file by the light of a single lamp an hour before dawn, in the room that Circle Lightfall had rented for him. There was a single hard-backed chair, a narrow bed, the lamp set on a small night table, and a space heater that he was careful to hang his coat away from. The walls were bare and white, and he didn't look at them.

"Theodora," he said, and the air in the room reverberated.

So that was her name. And invoking it this close to her house...he would be lucky if she was asleep enough not to notice.

Dante found himself wearing an unfamiliar smile. The picture, a black-and-white still, expanded, showed most of her face. It must have been snapped on a city street, because her long hair was being lifted from a slight breeze. Her eyes were large and luminous, even in black-and-white, and the shape of her mouth made him think of mischief. She had a long narrow nose, a flower-mouth, high sculpted cheekbones, and a gentle expression, even when she looked thoughtful.

"She just moved here four years ago," he said. "She's been bouncing around for a while, that's why the Crusade's missed her. Clever girl. Clever, clever girl."

He was talking to himself. He *never* talked to himself.

What was wrong with him?

He'd laid defenses and traps all along the block that held her house, and then he'd retreated to this little rented room to sleep. The Seeker's claw marks on his side ached dully, and there was a little bit of bruising there.

Maybe he was losing the trick of belief.

If that happened, he was dead in the water.

Dante touched the photograph, just along the curve of her chin. A pretty witch. A very pretty woman.

She had moved one step ahead of the Crusade. He could see that, from the itinerary outlined in the file. That was fantastic. But what was even more fantastic was how she had survived the stray predators wandering around. The odds of her surviving this long without a Watcher were like winning the jackpot on the only lottery ticket you'd ever bought in your life.

What had she been doing with a drunken, stinking normal on a city street after dark? And where had she put him? How had she not felt the Seeker? Had she felt it and simply ignored it? Not many things would dare to attack a Lightbringer…not in the vicinity of a Watcher. A Watcher's aura, like a red-black tornado, was a huge warning billboard. Only the desperately hungry—or the very powerful—Dark creatures would chance attacking a Watcher directly.

His weapons were all cleaned and re-consecrated, and he had caught a few hours asleep, ready to surface if the defenses were triggered. He was concentrating on the file, but the photo kept distracting him. Who was she looking at, her mouth turned up in a half-smile? The file said nothing about…

*What am I thinking?*

Dante read through the file one more time, committing it to memory. Birth date, favorite color, known Power, known associates, known addresses, bank accounts, and phobias. All useful information.

His eyes strayed back to the photo.

*She's beautiful*, he thought, in a kind of trance. *Why is she walking around alone?*

Then he shook himself, slapped the file shut and stared at it. It hit the carpet with a soft sound. He let some of the fury he was feeling trickle out, and the manila folder started to smoke and char along the edges. The pain crested, something he was used to, and he set his jaw and watched the flame begin to eat away at the paper.

He'd brought five other witches in to Circle Lightfall. He hadn't lost one yet. But none of them had…Well, none of them had even *seen* him. He'd just watched over them and kept them safe until a Circle witch could make contact and gently introduce them to the Circle.

Sometimes he thought that the lure they used to keep the Watchers busy—the chance of finding a Lightbringer who could ease the pain, a Lightbringer who could *touch* a particular Watcher—was nothing more than a pipe dream. But he'd seen some of the Watchers that had bonded to individual Lightbringers, and they seemed...well, happy. It was hard for a Watcher to contemplate happiness. They spent so much of their lives in training and combat as cannon fodder in the war against the Dark.

Hanson had lost a Lightbringer last year. He still wasn't the same. It was a blow to lose them. They were so few and far between. And so beautiful, such gentle souls.

The file was reduced to ash. His control was still good, none of the carpeting below was even touched.

Dante stood and stretched. His side hurt him. The Crusade was probably still out in the city, not to mention other predators, all of them potentially planning an attack. They weren't, really. They were too disorganized. But it helped to think like that, to prepare himself for every threat.

He would make contact with the witch Theodora today. It was too soon, and the Circle might not like it, but the Crusade wouldn't take kindly to the loss of a Seeker. It seemed that the Crusade was getting desperate lately—and no wonder. The Watchers had taken so many of the Lightbringers in, and the Dark was being balked at every turn.

Dante used the bathroom, grabbed his coat, and spent a few moments making sure it hung right. He made sure all his weapons were in their accustomed places and that the file was just a meaningless smudge of ash.

"Theodora," he said again, but quietly. Then he left the small room, locking the door and walking out into the gray, misty morning.

# Nine

"And a bright good morning to you, Theo," Elise said, her long fiery hair spilling over her shoulders. Today she was wearing a red velvet bustier and tight, crimson leather pants. The sun tattooed around her bellybutton peeked out, and the silver stud in her nose twinkled. "Didn't sleep well?'

Theo hung her coat up and sniffed. Elise had lit apple-cinnamon candles, and the entire store smelled like a baking pie. "Do I look tired?" she asked, sweeping her hair back over her shoulders. She should have braided it, but she had punched the snooze button one too many times, and as a result, came to work with wet hair and wearing a dark-green sarong and a black sweater. Normally she wouldn't wear black on a day when she felt tired, but she had been forced to grab the closest clothes. She was still wearing her grandmother's necklace, too, but that was habitual. She hardly noticed it.

"No, you look just like normal," Elise said. "Just a little white around the eyes, that's all. What's wrong?"

"I think I was—" Theo started to say, but just then, the bell over the door tinkled again.

The Magick Cauldron was a small store, but kept ruthlessly neat. There were books on the six bookcases set on the east wall, and the cash register was on a small glassed-in counter in the east as well, with the most precious books—the first editions and the texts that only the serious would be interested in—on the case directly behind it. A wooden door marked "Employees Only" led down to the basement storage space and a bathroom, as well as a small room that Theo had refurbished into a temple. The south wall was taken up with candles, incense, censers, candleholders, and scented oils. The western wall held statues and racks of cloaks and other things— a glass cabinet full of expensive jewelry, a rack of iron cauldrons, knives to be used as athames, and assorted other items. The north end of the store held the display window and the front door. Bells hung across the window on the other side of the door, and a small table, with three chairs that Suzanne sometimes used when she was reading tarot cards, sat in front of the window. There was also a small rack full of magazines and some free pagan publications. The floor was hardwood, and waxed with glitter in the wax so that it sparkled under the warm yellow light. Plants hung from the ceiling and graced the shelves, and a red-flowered orchid was set near the register. It had bloomed for a year now.

The bells jingled over the door, and Theo half-turned from the coat rack she was hanging her coat on. She smiled. Suzanne, a tall silver-haired woman with her braid twisted into a coronet atop her head, stood in the doorway and regarded Theo. "Hi, Suzanne. How are you—"

"Good morning, Theo," she said. "Mari will be along. Is there tea made?"

Theo felt her heart fall and then start to beat faster. "Why? Is something wrong?" For Suzanne to be up and about at this time of the day, and to have called Mari, who was busy studying for her finals...

Suzanne yawned delicately and stalked into the store. She was wearing yellow, as usual—a long fringed scarf and a canary silk suit, with a bright sunshine-yellow poncho made of chenille over the top. She walked behind the counter and then half-turned to survey the Cauldron. "Not precisely wrong, Theo darling, but I think something's up. The wind's uneasy today."

Elise's porcelain face changed slightly. "You know, when I lit the candles this morning, they were hissing blue. It took a while for them to get to normal." Her eyes were a wide clear green, not as dark as Theo's, and cat-tilted in her pretty, flawless face with an aquiline nose and wide generous mouth, which was usually smiling. "And none of the cats were out back. No sign of them when I put the dishes out this morning. I keep thinking that lightning's going to strike," she said, and looked nervously out the front window. It was a shock to see sarcastic Elise so serious. "Something's up."

Miraculously, Suzanne didn't scoff. "That's it exactly," she agreed, and Theo's jaw threatened to drop.

"I don't feel anything other than a sort of nervousness," she said. "Suzanne—"

"I'll start the tea," Elise interrupted, and hopped out from behind the counter and headed for the south wall. There was a small kitchen set there, behind the wall that the racks were hung on. "Theo, keep a watch out for Mari. Suzanne, are you going to throw the cards?"

"No," Suzanne said calmly. "I will *read* the cards. Watch out for Mari, Theo, and let's get started. I don't like this."

Theo felt her eyebrows nest in her hairline. She put her hands on her hips. "Just one moment, everyone," she said. "There's no need for all this. I just feel a little nervous, not enough to warrant any of this—"

"Theo, my dearest," Suzanne said, arching one gray eyebrow, "shut up. You don't feel it because it's directed at you, and it doesn't *want* you to feel it. So just let your friends help you, all right? There's a good girl." Suzanne folded her arms, her hazel eyes snapping with rare fire.

Theo threw up her hands. It was enough to make anyone laugh. "Oh, all right. I swear, the bunch of you are like a cattle-load of grannies harping at me. Go ahead and make the tea, Elise. I'll get my cards too, and we'll see who's right."

Just as Elise vanished into the kitchen, the bell over the door tinkled again, and Theo turned around. The greeting she was about to give died on her lips.

It wasn't Mari.

It was a tall man wearing a long, black leather coat. He had short crow-black hair that would have looked very precise and military, except that it was disarranged and gelled into short punk spikes. He had dark eyes—no, *black* eyes—over a sharp nose and a sinful mouth that quirked up at the corners, and wide shoulders and narrow hips. Theo actually took a step back. He topped six feet, and even with his hands in his pockets he looked like a man that nobody in their right mind would mess with. The size of his shoulders alone was enough to make Theo want to put the counter between her and him.

And his black eyes were fixed on her.

Theo felt heat rising to her cheeks. She stared at him and

something rose in her memory.

The man pacing by her house last night, silent and deadly. Theo narrowed her eyes. There was a faint flicker of energy around him, something that could—

Suzanne's arms were folded. "Welcome to the Magick Cauldron," she said, cautiously. "Can we help you find anything?"

The man didn't answer. He was staring at Theo, and she was staring back at him, blushing furiously. Her hands started to sweat. He was looking at her so intently that she could almost feel his eyes on her face, like fingers.

"Is it Mari?" Elise called from the kitchen.

Silence.

"Come *on*, guys," Elise called, and popped out of the blue and green leaf-patterned curtain that closed off the curtain. "Is it—*Hel-lo,* stranger." She sounded amused. "Can we help you? Please?"

That seemed to shake him out of his trance. He glanced over at Elise, and his face changed a little. Theo found her throat closing, and she clasped her shaking hands together. "Theodora Morgan," he said, and looked back at Theo. Or more precisely, at her boots. He didn't look back up at her face.

"That's me," Theo said. "Can I...Can I help you?"

She sensed a glamour, a spell to help people see only what they wanted to see when they looked at him. She narrowed her eyes, looking *under* the shield of magick, and saw that he was wearing knives strapped to his body, and a pair of bright silver guns. And to top off the utter impossibility, he had the leather-wrapped hilt of a *sword* poking up over his left shoulder.

*What, he just couldn't find anything else to wear this morning?* she thought, and found herself backing up.

Theo took two more startled steps back, her left hip hitting the glass cabinet that held the cash register. She barely noticed the flare of pain that caused. "What *are* you?" she asked, and saw something—a blush—rising up his clean-shaven cheeks. Blushing. A man who knew her name came strolling into her shop wearing guns, and he was *blushing*?

"You might not believe me," he said, and pulled something that looked like a business card out of his pocket. He offered it to her, still not looking up at her face. "I have several things to tell you, and I just..." He trailed off.

Theo couldn't back up any more. The glass cabinet was behind her. The air in the store stirred uneasily, the wards sensing her fear. How had he gotten through them, armed like that? "What are you?" she asked again. "Was that you, following me last night?"

He was still offering her the card. "All I can tell you right now..." He broke off and glanced at Suzanne. Theo looked back at Elise, who was leaning against a bookcase, grinning. "...is that you're in danger, and I'm here to help."

Suzanne drew herself up to her full height—she still only reached slightly past his chin. "I'll take that, thank you," she said, and plucked the card from his fingers. "Theo?"

Theo shook her head, her long, dark hair swinging. She opened her mouth to say something, but nothing seemed applicable.

He finally looked at her face again, and Theo felt the same chill she'd felt last night trace its way up her back. His eyes were flat and black and *cold*. Something lived in those eyes—something deadly.

Theo's entire body flushed with something that could have been ice or fire. She stared at him, her pulse racing thinly in her throat. She had seen enough danger to know that men with eyes like that were killers, and best left alone. As a matter of fact, he shouldn't have been able to get through the wards.

But his mouth quirked up into a half-smile, and she felt her heart thud against her ribs and then start hammering in her throat.

"Well," Suzanne said briskly, and the bell over the door jingled again.

"Sorry I'm late—" Mari piled in through the door, breathlessly, almost running into the tall man. He stepped aside, gracefully and silently, moving like a cat. This meant that he stepped very close to Theo, and she smelled him—iron and blood and a dark musky smell, the smell of something dangerous and sleekly muscled. Desperately, she put up her hands to ward him off, and he stopped, staring at her face. He looked as if he was about to say something, but he didn't speak. "Hot damn," Mari said. "Did I miss the party?"

"I'm sorry," he said softly to Theo, and she found that she believed him. He really did sound sorry. She could see the faint shadow of charcoal stubble on his cheeks and chin, and the arc of his cheekbone. Under the trench coat, he wore a black T-shirt and a pair of black jeans. There was no color on him except a faint blush high up on his cheeks. Was he really blushing? It didn't seem possible. "I mean it. I'm here to help."

"That's quite enough," Suzanne said crisply. "You can leave now, whoever you are. Theo—"

"I'm Dante," he said, still staring at Theo. He was very close, and she could feel the heat coming from him. Black eyes, and wide shoulders, and that heat. It was like a red-hot stove, a wall of heat wrapping around her.

She blinked and stared at him. Her heart was hammering so hard she was surprised nobody else could hear it. "I'm Theo," she said, blankly, and then felt a sharp flare of embarrassment. *Oh, Goddess, did I just say that? What kind of gormless idiot am I?*

His mouth quirked again, and he seemed to realize where he was again. "Nice to meet you, Theo. I'll be around." Then he turned, gave Suzanne a lazy salute. "Ma'am," he said, and then left the store, brushing past Mari, who stood there with her short blonde curls tumbling around her head. Her big blue eyes danced with merriment as she stepped aside to let him pass. The bell jangled pointlessly. Mari whirled and peered out the door to watch him walk away.

Theo let out a gusty sigh and slumped against the glass counter. "Wow," she said, and heard the stunned wonder in her own voice. "What was that?"

"Looked like a big heapin' helpin' of handsome to me," Elise said, glee evident in her tone. "Yum!"

"Circle Lightfall," Suzanne read from the card. "And a phone number. Nothing else. Theo? Have you ever heard of them?"

Theo shook her head and rubbed at her hip. She'd bruise there, unless she put some arnica and a healing charm on it. "Did you see the glamour on him?" Her voice shook, and Mari turned back from the door.

"He just vanished," she said, and her voice was shaky too. "Right off the street, while I was watching. I don't think I like this. I've been feeling queasy all day, and the rain seems to be...well, it's just whispering in a funny way. And now this. Theo, are you okay?"

"Did you see the weapons he was carrying, under the glamour?" Theo asked. "Or was I the only person that realized he carried two *guns* into this place?" Her voice hit a wavering note that didn't make her feel any better. She felt, in fact, shaky, like she needed to sit down.

"I noticed," Suzanne said. Her voice was thin and breathless. "Theo, you're pale. Let's go so you can sit down. Elise, bring the tea. Mari, turn the sign to 'closed' and lock the door."

"No," Theo said. "Customers. We need the—"

"Nobody's going to come until afternoon," Suzanne said. "I can tell. Don't argue with me, Theo. It puts me in a mood."

In short order they were all downstairs, sitting on the rugs in the dark temple. Elise snapped her fingers and the candles bloomed into life, a warm mellow light. Theo put her cold shaking hands around her tea mug and blew gently across the steaming liquid. Suzanne produced her tarot cards, wrapped in a hank of orange silk. Her necklace—a string of amber beads—gave back the candlelight.

The statue that Elise had carved—a Goddess with her arms upraised, a beautiful pregnant belly and curving breasts, and a slight smile on her gracious face—watched them with crystal eyes. The main altar underneath was hung with black and red for Samhain. Banks of candles were on each wall, and on the altars for the four directions. There was a plate of sugar cookies beneath the statue, Mari's latest offering. Theo had made the black and white candles gracing the main altar, and Suzanne's favorite black lace shawl was draped over the wooden Goddess, an antique mantilla affixed to her beautiful carved hair.

Theo shivered.

"Well," Elise said. "Do we need to cast a circle, or are we just powwowing?" She was holding her favorite mug, the one with red suns painted on it and a gold rim. The one that had to be handwashed, of course.

"Just powwowing, I guess," Theo said. "We have no idea what's going on. Suzanne, you saw his guns, didn't you?"

"Guns?" Mari said. "I was right next to him. I didn't see any guns."

"Of course not," Suzanne replied. She snapped the hank of orange silk, briskly. Her tone was businesslike, as if people walked around carrying guns in the Magick Cauldron every day. "He was glamoured. And glamoured well. Circle Lightfall." She held up the business card. "Mari, do you think you could get anything from this?"

Mari's blue eyes were thoughtful. "I could," she said, slowly. "With you three to anchor me, I wouldn't have to worry about slipping too far. Do you want me to?"

"Let's think about it," Suzanne said. She set her tea aside on the hardwood floor and started to shuffle her well-worn cards. "Theo, why don't you read too?"

Theo looked down at her hands. "I don't know," she said, softly. "I think I'm a little too upset to try right now. Let me have a little tea. I think he followed me home last night."

"What?" Suzanne's hazel eyes sharpened. "When? And why didn't you call me?"

"I saw Grody in the Creation and took him to Marla, so she could get him to the drunk tank. He'd gotten ahold of some gin. Anyway, as I was walking back, I heard…a scream, something awful. It frightened me, and I walked home, but I kept feeling as if someone was watching me. So when I got home, I left the lights off, and watched the street, and…Well, a man walked by, and I think it was him." Theo shrugged defensively. *That's right, go home. You're safe, I promise…*Had it been his voice, or had she just imagined it? "He didn't try to test my wards or anything like that, but it made me nervous."

"We could call the phone number on the card," Elise said. "Theo, honey, why didn't you call me? I would have come over."

"I didn't think it was that important," Theo said. Suzanne finished shuffling and laid out five cards.

They all looked.

"Oh, my," Elise said. "Girl, you are in trouble for sure."

*Knight of Swords. Three of Swords. The Tower. Three of Cups. Queen of Pentacles.*

Theo stared, the blood draining from her cheeks. "Oh," she said. "Well. I did ask for a little excitement in my life." The tea slopped against the side of her cup, a lacquered green mug with a pretty bamboo pattern on it.

"Be careful what you wish for," Suzanne said. "All right, ladies. Let's make some protection magick."

# Ten

*Well, that was the worst job you've ever done, you idiot,*
Dante told himself, hunching his shoulders and blending into
the rooftop. He was watching the front of the store below and
kicking himself at the same time. *She saw through your
glamour. Gods above and below, damn you for a fool, you've
scared her now. Your very first time making contact with your
witch and you've scared her to death.*

The morning wore on. They had put the "closed" sign up
and nobody even tried the door. Dante watched people walk
by, stop and look at the store, and then go on. The shop was in
a good location, plenty of foot traffic going to the boutiques
and the restaurants down the street…and he was thinking of the
deep lights in her green eyes. She had backed up against the
glass counter and banged her hip a good one. He had wanted to
reach out and stop her, but the way her eyes had widened and
her face had drained of all color had stopped him. He didn't
want to frighten her. The *last* thing he wanted to do was frighten
her.

The trouble was, he couldn't figure out the *first* thing he
wanted to do with her.

She would just barely reach his chin, and her long, dark,
wet hair had smelled of sandalwood. He had been able to smell
it as soon as he'd come in the door, and it had driven him to
distraction.

*What is wrong with me?*

It was early afternoon before the sign on the door turned to
"open," and the fire-haired woman came out. She walked with
a quick lilt, her chin up and her hair crackling like a banner on
the rainy wind. Dante's shoulders were wet, since there was
little cover from the rain here, only from prying eyes. Next the
tall older woman came out, glanced up and down the street,
and set off in the same direction. Her yellow scarf streamed
behind her in her own personal breeze. She had the unmistakable
lemon tang of an air-elemental, and Dante could see the

determination in her stride.

They had a full circle there. All four of them. It defied logic, but there they were. Magick was a highly illogical science.

"Theodora," he said to the wind, but the tall woman in yellow didn't stop. She went around the corner and disappeared. *What is wrong with me?* he wondered. It wasn't like him to be so…distracted. That could cost any of the women their life. He would have to call into Circle Lightfall and tell someone. Three Lightbringers and a Teacher, and only Dante to watch over them.

There was a slight scuffing sound to his right, and Dante whirled. Hanson landed on the roof and brushed his hands together, as if ridding them of dust. "Hey, old man."

"Honor," Dante said automatically.

"Duty. Cool, right? We get to Watch together." Hanson's blue eyes glittered. "I have the one in blue. She got here late this morning. Was supposed to be studying at the library, but they called her here, I guess."

"I made contact," Dante said. "Killed a Seeker last night, Hanson. You're right. The whole town is full of the Crusade."

Hanson's blue eyes narrowed. He glanced down at the store. "Damn," he said.

The shortest woman, the one with the flyaway tumbling blond curls and the big blue eyes, stepped out and glanced up the street. She shivered, pulled her sweater closer around her shoulders. She wore no coat, and her hair immediately rose on the cold wind, a blonde halo. "Three Lightbringers and a Teacher. The blue one's yours?" Dante watched as the short blonde walked slowly up the street. She seemed to be dawdling.

Hanson nodded. "Guess she's going back to the library. Wonder if they'll send another Watcher?"

"I don't know if they can spare another one." Dante scanned the street. "You'd better go. The Crusade's on alert now. They'll be pissed."

"Are you sure it's just the Crusade? Anyone else could be in town. *Gee, thanks, Hanson, for the nice surprise. We can team up and Watch together.* That would be nice to hear." Hanson stuck his hands in his pockets. "I never thought I'd live to see the day when I could sneak up on *you.*"

"You didn't sneak up on me. I'm focused, not distracted. And it was a created Seeker. Crusaders are the only ones crazy enough to do that." Dante felt his mouth trying to smile. "Better go watch your witch. If she comes back, come on up. This is a good spot."

"I've been watching the back of the store. Nothing there." Hanson stretched lazily, like a big cat. "Be careful, Dante. There's enough power in there to—"

"I know," Dante said. "And the Crusade's in town. Not to mention the usual nasties. The Brotherhood's been sniffing around, and the Thains."

"The Thains?" Hanson snorted. "Amateurs."

"Even amateurs can be dangerous. Get going." Dante was looking down at the shop, most of his attention on the glowing beacon it presented to anything with Sight.

"See you soon. Honor," Hanson said, and vanished over the edge of the building.

"Duty," Dante replied. "Absolutely."

If three of them were gone, then she was alone in the store.

*I am not going to go down there and frighten her again*, Dante thought, and saw Hanson edging down the street after the blue-eyed witch. The people on the street were starting to turn into a crowd. It was a crowd of afternoon shoppers.

Dante's boots hit the pavement in the alley, and he glanced around. The coast was clear. No sign of the Crusade. They didn't like to come out during the day—it was bad for the Seekers. Seekers were nocturnal anyway.

He watched as customers started to drift into the store. Teenage girls and older women, browsing and buying. The bell on her door jingled every time it opened, and most people left with a bag of something. Once she even accompanied a middle-aged woman with long brassy-colored hair and a peach business suit to the door, laughing at something the woman said. Dante's entire body leapt at the sound of that laughter.

The store had smelled like apple pies baking, and she smelled like sandalwood and green growing things. A green witch. A witch with green eyes.

Two young men, one of them with a Mohawk that stood up tall enough to give him an extra four inches of height, slid into the store. They left with a small paper bag and a pair of foolish grins. Dante suppressed another growl. They were just kids. What was *wrong* with him? He was a Watcher, not a—

The shop was empty. He saw her leaning on the glass case that held the ancient cash register, one hand absently rubbing her hip, while the wards sparked. She was testing them, making sure they were intact. Good practice. Probably trying to figure out how Dante had gotten past them.

Another young man, this one jittering and hugging the wall while running at top speed, slid into the shop. The shields on the shop turned a brilliant blue-green, and he was across the street before he knew it, pushing the door open and listening to the little bell jingle.

"—all right," his witch said, from behind the counter. "Just calm down and tell me what happened."

"I think he might die," the kid said, his teeth chattering. "There's a lot of blood."

"How did it happen?" she asked, and glanced up. Her eyes slid across Dante without really seeing him. She was doing something to the register with her left hand. "I'll be right with you, sir," she said, and then seemed to remember who he was. Her eyes widened, but she didn't seem frightened. The smell of magick hung in the air. So that was what they had been doing in here with the "closed" sign on the door. He couldn't tell exactly what had happened, only that an incredible amount of power had been raised and directed. Of course. Three Lightbringers and a Teacher…What *couldn't* they do? It was the magickal equivalent of a hurricane, at the command of these women. How had they managed to stay undetected so long?

The kid was swaying in place, his chest heaving. His eyes were dirty bruised holes in his face, scared beyond belief. He had lank dirty blond hair, and he wore a thin denim jacket, ragged jeans and wet sneakers. He was painfully thin, his elbows and wrists seeming too big for the rest of him. "I dunno. He just was choking and then his mouth started to bleed. He's jerking all around."

She locked the register, took the key and bent down, retrieving a small black canvas messenger bag. She stuffed the key into the bag. "All right," she said. "I'll come."

The boy sagged in relief. Teenage acne was just starting to develop on his face. "You mean it?" he asked, his voice breaking a little. Theo came around the edge of the counter and walked to the iron coat rack where her pea coat was hanging. She slid the strap over her head and snugged the bag across her body. Then she took the coat down and looked at Dante.

"Of course I mean it," she said. "I don't say things I don't mean. Sir, I have to leave now. The store will be open tomorrow."

"I'll go with you," he said, quietly.

"I don't have time to argue with you," she said, producing a set of keys from her pocket. "Out."

Abruptly, her voice became brisk, no-nonsense, and her eyes were dark and level. Dante held the door open for her, and the young man followed her out onto the street. Dante stepped out, the cold wind seeming to welcome him again. She locked the door with a key and then set off the same way that the thin young man had come from.

Dante followed her, falling into step slightly behind and a little to her right. "Where are we going?" he asked, watching the way the ends of her hair rose in the breeze. As long as he stayed calm and focused on her, the pain grinding inside his bones from the Darkness in him reacting to a Lightbringer was bearable.

The skinny young man ran up to her other side, and Dante suppressed the urge to grab the kid by the scruff of the neck and shake him away from her. "What's up, Theo, you got a boyfriend now?"

"I don't know, Hink," she said, dropping her head a little and looking at the pavement. "I just met him last night. He seems to want to come with us."

"He okay?" Hink asked, skipping away as Dante glanced at him. Theo was stretching her legs, setting a fast pace. Dante kept up with little trouble. The boy was almost running.

Theo glanced back over her shoulder at Dante. Her chestnut-colored hair streamed away on the freshening breeze. It was a dark, rich brown—a long mane that had coppery highlights when it wasn't wet. And he thought he could see faint tinges of moss-green to it, tree-colored hair.

"I think so," she finally said. "He wouldn't be able to come into the store if he wasn't."

"Good 'nuff," Hink said. "Any friend of yours, Theo."

"How much did he do, Hink? And where did you get it from?" Theo asked, changing the subject and quickening her stride again. They turned left at the end of the block.

"I don't *know*, Theo. I been clean for two weeks. I don't know where he got it from. He just went into the can, and when he never came out, I went in 'cause I had to piss, right? So I found him there shaking and blood coming out of his mouth—" Hink's voice broke again.

"He had it and he didn't share?" Theo said. "Come on, Hink." She didn't sound angry, only very sad. Dante's heart twisted inside his chest. She shouldn't have to be so sad, this kind patient witch with her dark green eyes. Anyone else, maybe, but not her.

The sun was going down soon, flashing under the clouds, and the light had a peculiar yellow cast to it. The rain was glittering like golden needles, caught in her hair.

"I don't know where he got it," Hink said, and this time there was a ring of frantic truth to it. "I been going to the methadone place, Theo. Honest. I don't know where he got it. Is he gonna die?"

"I don't know," she said, and she still sounded sad. And a little breathless. Dante said nothing, watching how she walked quickly, her hair lifting on the breeze and then dropping, moving with her. And also moving with the tide of green Power that seemed to be rising around her.

*What are you doing?* he thought, and then felt his mouth turn down at the corners. *I'm doing what I'm supposed to do. She's my witch, and I'm watching her. Watching over her.*

Theo glanced at the sky turning gold overhead, and she began to run.

# Eleven

The sloping stairs looped crazily up, and the tall man caught Theo's elbow when she almost fell. "Thanks," she said, and he nodded. What was he doing here? She didn't have time to ask.

"Up here. Ain't much, but it's home," Hink said, and ducked between boards that had been nailed over an empty doorway. She heard a wheezing rattle and would have tried to follow, squeezing between the boards, but the tall man grabbed her arm, his fingers gentle but iron-hard.

*He could break my arm without even trying,* Theo thought, and was grateful that he was being gentle. His black eyes were still distant, and she felt a small shiver. Why had she allowed him to come along?

His long coat lay against him like a cloak, and she swallowed. "What are you—"

"Just a moment," he said, and then went past her and wrenched at the top board. It tore free with an incredible ripping sound. He dropped it and proceeded to tear the bottom board free, too. "There," he said. "Easier."

"Thank you," Theo squeezed past him, ducking to get into the room beyond. The smell was awful—garbage and excrement, and the new smell of sickness. "Oh, Goddess," she said, and held her mouth open a little. She would get used to the smell—or not. It didn't matter.

Then she saw Billy and let out a sharp pained breath. He was lying on a dirty mattress someone had probably dragged up here. His skin was waxen-pale. He was agonizingly thin, and his eyes were rolled back, showing only their whites. His lank, greasy hair fell back onto the pillow, and his stick-arms were covered with sores and needle tracks. A black crust of foam dribbled from his lips. No, it wasn't black. It just looked that way in the uncertain light of the boarded-up windows. It was bloody foam that had dried on his lips. His face and chest were streaked with it. So were his hands and the mattress.

Theo went to her knees on the mattress beside him, shrugging out of her coat. The tall man—Dante—took it from her. "Theodora?" he asked, with a world of questions in his deep voice.

Theo ignored him. She took the boy's pulse, found it shallow and sluggish under her fingertips. He drew in another rattling breath. His lips were blue.

*It might be better just to ease him on,* the practical side of her whispered. *If he's this bad off he may be brain-damaged.*

She focused past that practical voice. *If the Goddess wanted him, She would have taken him,* she reminded herself. *I'm here to do what I was made to do.*

And under her fingertips the pulse stuttered and stopped.

She felt it then, the abused spark draining from the flesh that housed it, like a candle flame guttering in a draft. Hink said something. He was crouching on the other side of the mattress. Theo ignored him. She put her other hand on Billy's pale forehead and felt the healing begin, deep inside her, in that place that it always came from.

"Billy," she said. "You have to decide. I can't keep doing this for you." Her voice was gentle, and seemed to stop the dust in the air.

Billy had been meant for better things, at least until he had received his first taste of the needle. He had actually done some work for Theo at the Cauldron, putting up shelves and stacking boxes worth of stock. He had been a friend, of sorts, hanging around the shop, joking with Theo on long afternoons and meeting her at the Creation for coffee and long talks.

She exhaled, and the smell of green growing things began to fill the air, fighting with the smell of garbage. There was a sound like an organ note resounding in her bones, a huge thundering sound that filled her flesh with green light. It poured through her hands, and Theo was barely conscious of the tall man saying something.

The sound faded reluctantly, and when she opened her eyes again, the darkness was almost complete. Hink had a Sterno glowing, and a little light made the shadows inside the garbage-filled room dance. He was eating a Twinkie, sitting on the floor next to the mattress. He looked supremely confident in her ability.

Theo wasn't so sure.

She almost didn't want to take Billy's pulse, he looked so peaceful. But she did. It beat strongly under her fingertips, and his face was no longer pale wax but flesh and blood. "Ah." She rolled her shoulders back in their sockets. "He'll live," she said. The tracks were healing over, and the bruises and sores were mostly gone.

Hink's face went through glittering relief to fresh anxiety. He looked up at Dante, who stood at the side of the bed with his arms folded watching Theo. She glanced up and saw the tall man's eyes on her. He was holding her coat, and she shivered, suddenly cold all the way down to her bones.

He offered his hand. "Theodora." Just the one word.

She accepted his hand, and he pulled her to her feet as if she weighed nothing. He wrapped her coat around her, and Theo gave him a grateful look. Warmth started filtering back into her hands and feet. "Do you need money to feed him?" she asked Hink. "He should have some soup, lots of liquids. No more horse, okay?"

Hink shrugged. "I can't stop him, Theo. It's all I can do to stay off the horse myself. Got a kick like a mule, you know." He dug in his jacket pocket and came up with a joint. "You want some?"

"No, thanks. Do you want money?" Theo felt the tall man behind her, a silent presence. It felt oddly comforting.

"No, he'll just take it and go to a gallery." Hink shrugged. "I'll do some begging tomorrow or something."

Theo's heart twisted inside her ribs. "All right. Will you be all right?"

"I'll be okay, Theo. Thanks. I owe you one." Now he wanted them to go. He looked down at Billy and touched the other boy's forehead, smoothing his hair back. Theo felt a weary satisfaction. Love triumphing once again.

"Just stay off the horse, Hink," Theo told him. "I'll be going now."

"Thanks." Hink's eyes were bright and strange, tears

standing out in them. Theo swallowed what she wanted to say. "I mean it, Theo. You're a pal."

She nodded and pushed her hair back over her shoulders. The exhaustion rose from her feet and swamped her. The tall man's hand closed gently around her shoulder, and he said nothing. "Good night, Hink."

"Keep it cool, Theo."

She ducked back out of the small room and contemplated the hallway and the crooked stairs going down. Dante was right behind her, the warmth of him coming through her coat. "Walk near the wall," he said quietly, his hand on her shoulder. "The stairs are more solid there. Do you want me to go first?"

Theo shrugged. Now that she was standing up, the fatigue began to beat in her head.

"How do you get home after these sessions?" Dante asked. "Do you usually just stumble along?"

"Sometimes I call a cab," Theo said, dryly. "Most of the time I just walk. Do you usually follow strange women into abandoned buildings?"

"No," he said. "Only you. Come on, then."

He led her slowly down the stairs, stopping every once in a while to reach up and hold her hand, guiding her down the steps. It was pitch-dark, but he moved as confidently as if it was daylight. "Are you going home, or back to the shop?" he asked.

"I should go back to the Cauldron," she answered, and swayed on the steps. "They'll be worried about me. They always are. And you...What *are* you? You can see in the dark, can't you?"

He caught her shoulder, guided her down the last few steps to solid ground. The stairs stopped their groaning and squeaking. The rest of the building was apparently deserted and as quiet as a graveyard. Except that in Theo's opinion, graveyards weren't all that quiet. "I can," he answered, quietly.

"Are you Kine?" she asked. "You don't smell like a Kine, or act like one."

"You know about the Kine? Oh, of course you do. No, I'm not a shapeshifter. I'm something else. There's some broken

glass, be careful…and a beam, you could trip on that. Here."
His hands were at her waist. He picked her up as if she weighed
nothing, and then set her down again.

"I'm all right," Theo said. "I won't break. Look, I want to
know—"

"In a little while, Theodora. Let's get you out of here, all
right?" He sounded a little surer of himself now. He had a nice
voice, she decided. Restful, like the brush of velvet against
skin. Maybe he wasn't as scary as she thought.

Then again, he was carrying *guns*. "It's Theo," she said.
"That's what everyone calls me. You might as well call me
that too. And you're…Dante?" Her voice bounced off the
concrete floor and the indifferent walls. She remembered that
this building had once been a hotel, and they were on the ground
floor now, making for the door that had been jimmied open. It
was a good place to hide, until it was demolished or refurbished.
Billy and Hink must have been here for a while, for their room
to be so full of rotting scraps and other things.

"Dante," he agreed.

"Where's your Virgil?" she asked, and swayed on her feet
again. The ground was rocking oddly, like it did sometimes
when she was very tired. Dante had her elbow, steadying her.
His hand was warm, and she could feel it through her coat. It
was oddly comforting.

"I don't need a guide through hell," he replied shortly, and
then pushed the door open and looked outside. Faint and
welcome light from a street lamp set on the other side of the
chainlink fence showed the same weedy vacant parking lot
that they had run through to get here. "Here we are. It feels
relatively safe." The air was chillier now, no rain but a promise
of cold wind brushing at Theo's cheeks.

"Why were you following me last night?" Theo asked.
Her voice seemed to come from very far away. Too little sleep,
no dinner, and a major healing, not to mention the protection
spell they had all worked that morning, meant that she was
weaving on her feet. Suzanne had insisted on protection for
Theo. The Knight of Swords was a powerful protective force,
but the Tower—change, disruption, violence—also loomed in

Suzanne's cards. The trouble was Theo couldn't trust that Dante was the Knight of Swords, even though he was literally carrying a sword. The cards often weren't that literal. Suzanne said that he was and Theo trusted her, but…

"Someone has to look after you," he returned. "Looks like I'm nominated. Here, lean on me."

She did, too tired to really care what he was doing. If he had wanted to hurt her, he could have very easily done so while she was deaf to the world with her hands on Billy and the green light roaring through her. He helped her across the uneven, cracked pavement and pushed the chainlink fence aside as if it was made of paper. Metal screeched and snapped. "Be careful," she said. "If someone finds out Hink and Billy are here—"

"Not my problem," he said. "How often do you do this?"

"As often as I need to," Theo heard herself reply sharply. "How often do *you* do this?"

"As often as I need to," he echoed. "Relax, little witch. I'm just asking if you make it a habit to go into abandoned buildings with heroin addicts. That boy would have died, you know. Might have been better off, too."

"If the Goddess wanted him, She would have taken him," Theo repeated. "I don't get to choose where I'm called. We've always healed the sick, or so Suzanne tells me."

"Suzanne. The Teacher." He was guiding her down the sidewalk, going slowly. She was leaning against him, her head resting as close to his shoulder as it could get. He was a little too tall for that, but somehow he managed. "Did she teach you how to do…what you do?"

"No…" The word trailed off on a long breath of air. Theo realized blankly that she was walking with his arm over her shoulders, as if she had known him for a long time. His coat smelled like leather, and faintly like iron and rain. It was a comforting smell. "I learned what to call it from books, but I've always known I was different. Suzanne's just my most recent teacher. I've moved a lot, learning from anyone who could teach me…and I always knew when to move." She yawned. "I'm tired."

"A major healing after a major spell," he said, and she thought how deep and restful his voice was. "It's surprising you're still awake. I'll find us a cab or something. Save your strength."

Theo was about to tell him that she could find her way back to the Cauldron on her own when she passed out.

# Twelve

He tapped on the glass door and had the satisfaction of seeing the elegantly tall woman in yellow whirl towards the door, her eyes wide. She had an athame in her right hand and a piercing look in her hazel eyes. He would be willing to bet that the ritual knife was humming and vibrating with power.

The blond witch unlocked the door and stood back, and he carried Theo inside, shouldering the door open. The bell jangled discordantly. Dante felt a brief burst of pain—three Lightbringers and a Teacher, and the Darkness in him rising. He shoved it down, and it went, snarling. The feel of Theo in his arms helped. If it wasn't for her, he would be half crippled with pain.

It was a vicious circle. The more pain, the more the Darkness inside him fed on the pain, and the more powerful it became. The more powerful it became, the more it hurt to be near Lightbringers...except his dark-haired witch. She could *ease* his pain.

"Where were you? Is she okay? What did you do to her? Where did you—" The blond witch's blue eyes were full of sparks. She wore a blue sweater with a hole in it and a pair of jeans, and her feet were bare. Dante glanced at her, evaluated her as no threat, and looked outside. Hanson was nowhere in sight. He was almost certainly watching. Hanson's witch was here and not likely to go anywhere soon, so Hanson was here, too.

"Some kid named Hink came here with a sob story about an overdose," Dante said shortly. Theo's dark hair lay over his shoulder. He had been able to smell her sandalwood perfume while he walked. "Get her some tea, something hot and sweet. She just yanked a junkie back from the long walk. Do you have any food?"

"I'll go get some—" the blond witch started, and Dante jerked his head up.

"No. Go to the door, open it up, and say that you need

Hanson. Got it?" Dante tried to keep the growl out of his voice, but he didn't succeed. "He'll run for food and—"

There was another tap at the door. Dante turned and saw Hanson standing there with a bag full of Chinese food cartons. His hair glinted in the light, an icy blond with streaks of gold. "Good," Dante said. "Let him in."

The blonde looked at the Teacher, who pursed her lips and nodded. "Go ahead," the tall, slender silver-haired woman said. "He's carrying food, so we might as well get *something* out of this mess."

The blonde nodded, ran to the door, threw the lock and let Hanson in.

"I see my instincts are still on," Hanson said. He tore his eyes away from the blonde and looked at Dante, a head-to-toe appraisal. "What happened? You look—"

"Who was it?" The Teacher interrupted him, her eyes full of fire. "Which junkie? Elise, get some tea, and bring my hazel wand. It's got a charge in it. Mari, get plates and cups and chopsticks. You, whoever you are, lock that door and bring that food in." She sounded like a battlefield general. "You, tall one, bring Theo downstairs."

Theo made a low sound, her forehead wrinkling. Dante glanced down at her and saw her eyelids fluttering. The red-haired witch and the blonde both obeyed the Teacher without question, and Hanson had the sense to lock the door and turn back to the neat little store. "Some kid named Hink," Dante replied. "The patient's name was Billy. Bad overdose, ma'am, maybe the worst I've ever seen."

"How many, exactly, have you seen? And Theo dropped everything, closed up the store, and ran. What were you doing there?" The Teacher motioned for him to follow her, and he did, still carrying Theo. When she opened the "Employees Only" door to reveal a staircase, he was pleasantly surprised. And when he carried Theo downstairs, careful not to bump her head against anything, he was even more pleasantly surprised.

The small temple was exquisitely maintained, the main altar set in front of the red-draped south altar held a beautiful wooden Goddess draped with black lace. The Power in the air here was so strong that some color washed back into Theo's cheeks. The aching along Dante's ribs from the Seeker last night gave one last flare and subsided.

The Darkness beating behind his heart growled and went back to sleep.

The Teacher went to a small cabinet under the West altar and drew out some silk floor pillows. "Here. Set her down. What were you doing when Hink came here?"

Dante lowered Theo gently, making sure her head was pillowed safely, and looked up at the Teacher. "Watching over her," he said, shortly. "It's what I'm supposed to do. Three Lightbringers and a Teacher, it's a wonder you haven't attracted more attention."

The tall woman drew herself up. "*Lightbringers*," she said, and her tone had changed. It was definitely colder. "I've heard that terminology before. Who *are* you?'

"Dante," he said. "And you must be Suzanne. Pleasure to meet you."

"I can't say the same," she snapped. Indeed, she didn't look pleased at all.

The two witches—blonde and red, both vibrating with Power—came tripping blithely down the stairs. "How is she?" the blonde asked, her blue eyes large and worried.

Hanson was right behind them, his icy blond hair slightly disarranged. "I've trapped the front of the store," he said shortly. "I think there's a Seeker out there, Dante. Point of fact, I think there's more than one. We've got four civvies to take care of."

"Great," Dante said. "Are we going smoke-out or are we going to—"

"Suzanne?" Theo said, sounding groggy. Her eyelids fluttered again. Dante glanced down.

"—or are we going to play Masada?" Dante finished.

"My vote goes for smoke," Hanson said. "Then again, I've always been impulsive. I got you some prawns. Vegetarian for you, ladies—"

The Teacher went down to her knees by Theo and stroked

her forehead. "Theo," she said, softly, "are you all right?"

"I must have...passed out," Theo said. The other two witches started to divvy up the food, the blonde thanking Hanson in a clear, low voice. The redhead passed a finely-crafted hazelwood wand with a tiger's eye set on the tip to the Teacher, who passed it to Theo. She folded her hands around it and sighed. "How did I—" She sounded disoriented.

"Apparently, Mr. Dante carried you here." The Teacher sounded grim. "Theo?" There was a wealth of questions in the word.

Theo nodded, blinked. Her eyes were dark, and she looked a little pale. Dante squashed the urge to stroke her cheek. "He's all right, Suzanne. If he wanted to hurt me, he could have done so while I was healing Billy. Poor Billy, he's going to die soon, and I can't do anything about it." She closed her eyes again. Tears leaked out from under her long, dark eyelashes, which fanned against her sculpted cheekbones.

"Here's some tea, Theo," the blonde said. "Can you sit up?"

Dante found himself holding Theo's shoulders gently and propping her up so she could take a long drink of tea. It was made very strong and sweet, and she grimaced after she drank a long draft of it. Her throat moved as she swallowed, and he found himself looking at her eyelashes and the charming little tip of her nose. And the color coming back into her cheeks.

"Take it easy. You put yourself almost into shock, little witch," he said. "You should drink more of this, and eat something."

"God, Suzanne," the redhead said, her eyes sparkling. "He sounds just like you." She popped a potsticker in her mouth and wriggled her eyebrows.

The Teacher sniffed disdainfully. "I don't know who these men are," she said frostily, "or why they feel the need to enter our sanctuary armed to the teeth. It would do you good to exercise some caution, Elise."

"Oh, come on," Elise replied, tossing her head. "They're *hunks,* Suzanne!"

"Fair face may hide foul heart," the blonde broke in,

accepting a bowl of chow mein from Hanson. "Thanks, mister. Who are *you*?"

"Name's Hanson. I'm a Watcher, sent to watch over you." Hanson sounded uncharacteristically somber, his sharp pale face set and straight. "That over there is Dante, sent to watch over your friend. He's never lost a witch, but I think we've lost him as a Watcher."

"Time out," the redhead said. "Does anyone mind explaining some of this to me? And using some really small words?" She flicked her fingers, and the candles on the main altar ignited with little puffs of flame. "I'm getting a little impatient here."

Dante's eyebrows wanted to rise. That casual power impressed him—not as much as Theo's gentle healing, but it was still impressive. He would bet that Theo could light a candle or two, but wouldn't be so blatant about it.

"First things first," Suzanne said. "Eat, if you're sure it's not poisoned. Save that soup for Theo, and I want you to eat every last drop of it, young woman. You know better than to drain yourself like that."

"I don't have any control over the healing," Theo said. Dante could feel the fine shivers running through her body, her slim shoulders shaking just a little. She seemed not to notice that he was holding her up. "It comes through me. I don't control it."

"You should learn some control." The Teacher cast a critical eye over the assorted foodstuffs and the dark-green bowls and plates that the other two witches had brought. "Well. And how did you know what we usually order from Wu Fong's, young man?"

Hanson picked up a pair of plastic chopsticks and a container of pork fried rice. "I just asked what you usually got and added my own favorites onto it. You're welcome, by the way."

Dante glanced around the small temple. He would feel if the defenses upstairs were breached, but he still felt uneasy being in this blind a bolthole. On the good side, it gave an attacker only one possible avenue to exploit. On the bad side, they could be trapped down here with decidedly non-magickal weapons. The Crusade had been known to use grenades.

Hanson met his eyes. "It's crawling with Crusaders out there," he said grimly. "Someone must have stirred up *that* anthill. Think it was you, oh master of discretion?"

"I killed it quietly," Dante replied. "You're the one wandering around buying Chinese food."

Theo finished her tea. The hazel wand lay in her lap, sparking with Power that was slowly leaching into her, replacing what she'd expended on healing.

Dante suppressed a shudder at the thought of her dealing with that filth and degradation alone. How many times had she done that—or gone into even worse places to heal someone? And how would she have made it home from that? He watched her lower the tea mug and was struck by how graceful her fingers were. She was wearing amber rings, he noticed, and a plain silver band on her right index finger. A moonstone was on her left middle finger. Her earrings swung against her cheeks—today they were plain silver Celtic crosses. She was wearing an antique silver necklace set with a ruby as big as a silver dollar. And the power that shone through her.

"Killed what?" the blonde witch asked.

"One thing at a time," Dante said. "Theo? Are you all right? Can you eat something?"

She blinked and then looked up at him. "You," she said, sounding surprised. "Did you carry me?"

"I did," he said. "You lost consciousness, and I didn't want to drag you on the pavement. So I carried you."

"Did you strain anything, carrying me?" she asked, and there was a faint smile on her face. She blinked again, and her dark-green eyes met his.

"I don't think so," he said, helplessly. He saw the way a stray silken strand of her dark hair fell forward over her face and wanted to brush it back. His fingers actually ached to touch it. "You were tired." If he made his hand into a fist, the aching would go away, but it might frighten her. So he simply sat frozen, still holding her up. Her black sweater was soft.

She nodded. "Thank you. I would have made it back here,

but…thank you."

He shrugged. "Have something to eat," he said, desperate to change the subject. "It will help."

The Teacher had some egg flower soup in a bowl. "Here. All of it, mind you. *All* of it."

Theo nodded, took the bowl, and sipped at it. "I can sit up," she said, and swayed a little. "I can."

"Sure you can," Dante said. He had almost forgotten the rest of them. He braced her shoulders so that she could sit up. "Just drink some more soup. The Teacher's right. You need your strength back."

"Wow," the redheaded witch said. "Third time's the charm."

"Apparently," the blonde laughed and picked up a potsticker. "*Now* can we get some answers?"

Dante opened his mouth to start explaining when he felt it. The air turned thick and cold and the defenses set on the shop shivered. Theo flinched, and Dante stroked her shoulders with a comforting touch.

Hanson stiffened and set down his bowl. He met Dante's eyes and nodded. "Guess it's time to go to work, old man. Ladies, excuse us."

"Stay here," Dante told Theo, softly. He didn't want to scare her. "Something's outside, and we'll go clear it. All right?"

Her eyes sharpened. "What is it? And what do you mean, clear—"

Then all three of the witches—and the Teacher—flinched. Something hit the shields on the front of the shop with an almost physical *thud*. Dante propped Theo up on a pillow and flowed to his feet, the pain beginning inside his bones. The Darkness inside him was rising, and it hurt to be this close to the other Lightbringers. That was good. The pain would wake him up, snap him out of this…whatever it was that was distracting him so badly. It was his job to be cold and competent, to ensure her safety.

"Seems like we arrived just in time," Dante told her. "Look, there's a group—the Crusade—and all they want to do is kill people like you. Lightbringers, those with the Power. They're not the only ones, but they're the worst. They were given their marching orders in 1491 by Pope Innocent VIII. The Malleus Malleficarium had been written, but one of Innocent's cardinals made the case for a military order, empowered to act in secrecy—"

There was another shuddering impact against the shields, and Theo paled, slumping against the pillows.

"History later," Hanson snarled, from the stairs. "Come *on*, Dante!"

"Go," the Teacher said. "I'll take care of them."

Dante hesitated another moment, and then followed Hanson. He waited until he reached the top of the steps to take his guns out. "Is there a back door?" he asked.

"You mean you didn't look? Yes, there is. Damn it, Dante, can you fight or are you going to act like—" Hanson's face was a mask of rage. Dante was suddenly, overwhelmingly furious himself. The rage would give him strength.

"I'll fight," he growled. "Let's go."

# Thirteen

Theo pulled up her knees. Suzanne settled a soft blanket over her. "There, there, child. We're in the hands of the Goddess. The shop is well-warded, and I'm sure those men will..." She trailed off, her hazel eyes suddenly dark. "I've heard that term before, *lightbringers.*"

"What do you know?" Theo asked, accepting another bowl of soup with a nod of thanks. "Suzanne, he came in the door right after Hink burst in here and followed me down to their squat without a word." Her gaze sharpened as she caught the look exchanged between Elise and Mari. "And what do you mean, third time's the—"

There was another impact, this one greater than the first two, so hard that the walls shook. *I hope the window doesn't break*, she thought, and grimaced. The wards stretched, but didn't break. Yet. Another few hits like that...

"We...um, well, we want you to be happy," Mari said, lamely. "You're so *lonely*, Theo. So we...we just asked. In accordance with free will—"

Theo's eyebrows raised. So the pink quartz and rose oil had been for a bring-me-love spell. "You two cast a spell and *this* is what happens?"

"If you don't mind." Suzanne's tone was frosty. "I have heard of people who use the term 'lightbringer.' They are affiliated with an organization called Circle Lightfall, very mysterious. I have heard a very little bit about these *Watchers*. They're dangerous. Death follows them around, and they seem to follow women with Power."

"Are they really dangerous?" Elise asked. "Do I need to get ready to kick some ass?"

"They don't seem that dangerous," Theo said. "He carried me here. It must have been a good twelve blocks."

"They are said to be warriors against the Dark. We don't know anything about them," Suzanne said. "You said he followed you home last night?"

"I'm not certain it was him," Theo said, even though she was. "And he stood there and waited while I healed Billy." She sipped at her soup, her eyes distant. She'd laid the first layer of protections on the shop herself, and then Elise, then Mari, then Suzanne. Then all four of them had applied three layers of warding, so they were probably safe. There had been no more attacks on the wards, and the layers of energy on the shop had begun to smooth out, humming slightly.

So they were safe. But if they couldn't leave the shop...And what if something happened to Dante or the other man? "And I can't *believe* you cast a love spell on me."

"It wasn't a love spell," Elise said. "It was just a little...just asking for you to have a little happiness. Just to bring someone nice into your life."

"Oh, Goddess...And 'nice' means men armed with guns?" Theo sipped at the soup again. It was good, and she was starving. "So do we trust these men, or do we bar them from the shop?"

"I don't know," Suzanne said heavily. "I don't know what's attacking us. Perhaps I should go up and take a look."

"No!" Mari said suddenly, her blue eyes wide and dark. "No, don't go up there, Suzanne. Let them do what they have to do." She was holding another potsticker. "At least it's not like last time, when those awful things were attacking people."

"Why are we just sitting here calmly having dinner while those two guys go out and do God-knows what? How do we know they haven't planned this? How do we know that anything they say is true? And why—" Elise seemed at a loss for words. Sparks snapped off her long hair and died in the air surrounding her. Her aura was crackling with anger.

"Elise," Theo said, and set down the soup. She held out her hand. "We're sitting here calmly having dinner because three strikes against the shop's wards haven't even dented them yet. We can afford to sit here and save our strength in case the wards do break."

Elise's fingers met Theo's. Elise's red hair smoothed down, and the sparks stopped. "And they haven't done anything to harm us yet," Theo continued. "The wards would have kept them out if they meant us any harm."

Mari moved closer, and Theo held out her other hand. Mari took it, and she offered her other hand to Suzanne. "I don't like this," Mari said quietly. "There's too much about this we don't know."

"So we let them explain," Theo replied. "And we call this Circle Lightfall and check them out. It would be hard for anyone to lie to us without *one* of us knowing. We're powerful, Mari. We know that. We're in Her hands."

"In Her hands," Suzanne echoed. She took Elise's hand,

and then Mari's, so that they were all sitting in a circle, the forgotten dinner steaming on the floor.

The power hummed through them, a completed circuit.

"Well," Suzanne said. "I think we should be careful. I think any organization might want to use us for their own purposes, and until we know more, we should be very cautious."

Theo nodded. "I agree. Mari?"

"I agree too." Mari nodded. Her face had smoothed out.

"I can get behind that," Elise said. A spark snapped in front of her, and her face eased. "If they're lying to us, I swear I'll—"

"Careful, Elise," Theo cautioned. "Remember, what's spoken in Circle has power."

"I'll be very upset," Elise finished, as if she had intended to say that to begin with. "Now, you should eat, Theo. As long as they've stopped banging on the front of the store, it would be a shame to waste the food."

"Yeah." Mari smiled. "At least we didn't have to pay for it this time. A nice guy, buying us dinner."

"True." Theo smiled, and then sighed. The exhaustion came back, swamping her. "I should eat something. I'm starting to fade, and if anything happens, we'll need me to—"

"I couldn't agree more," Suzanne said firmly. "Eat, ladies. It looks like it's going to be a long night."

Theo smiled, and they broke the Circle. She picked up her soup again. "It certainly seems that way." She thought of Dante's eyes, black and fathomless, and the way he had been looking at her. Almost *hungrily*. She shivered a little, sipped at the hot soup. "Is there any stir-fry in there?"

# Fourteen

Dante blinked blood out of his eyes. "Hanson?" he called, covering the alley entrance.

"Got it." Hanson streaked past him. "Cover me."

Dante cursed. Hanson was taking a chance. He followed, his boots pounding on the concrete. *Two Knights,* Dante thought. *Four Seekers. And a Master. They're throwing everything but the kitchen sink.* His shoulder ached where he'd driven it into the first zombie Knight's midsection. Hanson had killed one, and Dante had stunned his, strung him up, and left him there, having no time to properly dispose of it. Now the Master was fleeing, with the last Seeker in tow.

*Fleeing—or setting a trap?*

The Master was in view now, a slim man-shape wearing the traditional white vest under a mid-thigh black coat. He turned and had his sword out. The Master had to be close to have any kind of control over a zombie. The zombies weren't too good at swordplay, just good at using the Seekers to hunt down defenseless Lightbringers. Speaking of Seekers…

Dante cast a glance around for the Seeker and located it halfway up the alley wall. *Tricky, tricky—*

The thought that this *thing* was only here to hunt Theo down and kill her drew a red haze over Dante's eyes. He leapt, preternatural speed and strength turning him into a blur, and met it as it began its own leap for Hanson's back.

Metal clashed and slid. Hanson let out a yell. Dante ripped the back of the Seeker open, his right hand caught in the thing's shadowy mane, his left full of black rune-chased steel. It wasn't the neatest cut in the world, but it ripped the Seeker loose of the physical world and scattered it.

Dante hit the concrete of the alley, rolled, and came up on his feet with his sword out and humming with scarlet Power.

Hanson twisted his own sword in the Master's middle. "Not on my watch." Hanson said through gritted teeth. "Not on *my* witch."

"Hanson!" Dante advanced, slowly. "Are you—"

"Just scratched." Hanson twisted the blade a final time and withdrew it, turning in the same motion and gaining momentum, and then his sword was a solid arc of silver. The Master's head hit the concrete with a thump. The smell of blood filled the air. One more body that wouldn't be reanimated for the Crusade's holy war. One more soul released. "One Master, two Knights and four Seekers. Did I miss something?"

"I hope not," Dante said. "Take care of that, and I'll go back for the second Knight. I left it hanging off a six-story drop. If it can wriggle free of the binding, it'll be very uncomfortable. Sudden deceleration." Dante's lips stretched to show his teeth. "You're bleeding."

"So are you. Good thing you know a healer." Hanson shook the black blood from his sword. "Where do they find them nowadays, do you think? The bodies for the zombies?"

"I don't know," Dante said. "Guess there can't be that many Masters around these days. Jack Gray and Piers both bagged Masters in the last month."

"Good." Hanson's shoulder was bleeding through his coat, and he had a raw-looking scrape on his cheek. "Go get the zombie. I'll take care of cleanup. Meet you back at the shop."

"All right," Dante agreed. "Honor, brother."

"Duty. Good fight."

It was a long way to the place where he had left the zombie hanging over a six-story drop. Dante felt the blood sliding out of the slice along his hairline. He would present a fine picture when he came back to the shop. Maybe Theo would feel sorry for him.

# Fifteen

The food wasn't even cold by the time the bell over the door jangled. Theo looked up at Suzanne. "It's them," she said. "So a locked door doesn't mean anything to them." She was leaning on the pillows with her legs drawn up, her eyes heavy with exhaustion. All she wanted to do was go home and sleep. Mari took a ladylike sip of tea. "Well, I checked it," she said, practically, "So we know it *was* locked."

"Polite of them to act like it *does* mean something," Suzanne said stiffly. "Theo, dear, just rest."

"I think this is going to be a very long night," Elise said. "You should have taken a nap."

"Will you both quit fussing at me?" Theo answered, irritation coloring her voice. She closed her eyes and counted to ten. It wasn't like her to be so snappish. It was unsettling to have a tall man with black eyes looking at her so intently, following her home…and leaving while something battered at the wards she had spent so long reinforcing. Just like a knight riding off to war.

The Knight of Swords.

When she opened her eyes, she heard boots on the stairs leading down to the temple. Elise was looking at the doorway, her fingers tense, one hand slightly lifted. Crackling static outlined her hand. Of all of them, Elise was the best of the offensive magicks. She was also a scrapper, mostly because her band played regularly in bars. Elise had once launched herself off the stage into a bar fight, lips drawn back, fists flying, and gotten a broken nose by the time the dust settled. Theo had set it for her, so there was only a slight appealing crookedness to her beautiful aquiline nose. Elise had gone right back to the stage and played the rest of the show with a bloody face and a fierce Valkyrie grin.

The blond man appeared. He was bleeding from his shoulder and limping, and Theo and Mari both gasped. There was a raw-looking patch on his cheek, too, and he was moving a little stiffly. "Good God," Elise said, rocketing to her feet. "What the—"

"We've got some time to answer some questions now," the blond man said. "Do you have a first-aid kit?"

"Elise, go get the first-aid kit," Suzanne said.

Theo made it to her feet, the blanket falling to pool on the floor. "What happened?" she asked. "Come here and sit down."

Dante appeared behind the blond man. His face was covered with blood, and his black eyes were blazing with something that made the air in the room go cold. It was as if the entire room resounded with his presence, like a huge bell being stroked until it sounded. He seemed even taller now, and, impossibly, more dangerous.

Mari let out a short, soft sound. She backed away, towards the main altar, but Theo took two steps forward. Her hands came up. Elise was already running up the stairs to get the first-aid kit.

"No," Dante said, harshly. "Don't touch me."

Theo stopped, her hair falling forward over her face. She shoved it back. "What?" *He can't have said that.*

"Don't. Touch. Me." He actually took a step back, his eyes dropping to look at the hardwood floor. The blood on his face was too red in the candlelight. "Dangerous."

Theo's hands started to ache. "But," she began.

"He means it, lady witch," the blond man said. "He's in a temper, best to let him calm down on his own. It hurts, you see." His own eyes were dark. He looked at Mari, who was standing by the altar, one hand braced against it. He *stared* at her, as a matter of fact.

Theo had to put her hands behind her back. They were throbbing with Power. The need to heal was beginning to hurt. "But I'm supposed to *help*," she said. "It's what I do." She could feel the prickles in her fingertips begin to run up her arms.

"Give him a few moments," the blond man said. "Can I sit down? I'll take some of that chow mein now, if you don't mind."

"Theo," Suzanne said, "perhaps you should get some tea

for our guests?" The older woman's mouth turned down at the corners. "And then we should settle down and have a nice long talk." Suzanne's eyes were cool and worried.

Theo barely heard her. She was looking at Dante's face, grim under its mask of blood, and the way he was favoring one broad shoulder. She didn't even realize that she had stepped up next to him, and that he had backed away from her, until his wide shoulders hit the wall between the door and the west altar, hung with blue and decorated with seashells and blue candles that Theo had made. She looked up at him, and lifted her hand. It was glowing dully, an emerald green. "Dante," she said.

As if she knew him.

He finally looked at her. "No, Theo," he said. His eyes were dark holes in his face. Theo's hands ached with the need to touch him. "Please. Don't. It will hurt you. You're still drained from the other healing. Don't worry about me."

"What happened to you?" she asked. "Talk to me, *tell* me."

"Just a scratch," he said. "Nearly dislocated my shoulder. It's all right, Theo. It's not the worst I've ever had."

"But *why?*" she asked. "What did you do? Who was trying to get into the shop?" She could see the blood drying in his short black hair and soaking into his coat.

"Let me sit down and get bandaged," he said. "And maybe have something to eat, all right? Please?"

The sight of this wounded man, asking her politely if he could sit down, brought Theo partly back to her senses. "Fine," she said, suddenly, acutely embarrassed. Her cheeks felt hot, and she stepped back just as Elise returned with the first-aid kit. "I'll go get some tea. Then I expect to have all my questions answered."

"Every single one," Dante said. "I promise."

Oddly enough, that made Theo blush even harder. He was staring at her again. As if he couldn't take his eyes away. His black, black eyes. Why did he have to be so *big?*

The blond man was already sitting down, eating like a starving man would eat—if a starving man had manners. Theo glanced around the room.

Suzanne was standing by the main altar, wrapping her yellow silk scarf around her neck. She looked thoughtful. Mari had taken the first-aid kit from Elise and was on her knees beside the blond man, saying something in a low voice. Her blue eyes were wet with tears, and she ran a hand back through her tumbled golden curls while she opened the kit.

Elise had stalked to the South altar and was lighting a stick of incense. "Goddess, give me patience," she said, pitching her voice loud enough to be heard, even from Theo's position by the stairs. "I'm trapped in a bad action movie. This is the part where we bandage up the nice warrior princes and hear a little bedtime story. Go and get some tea, Theo, the suspense is *killing* me."

Theo nodded. "Very well," she said, and turned on her heel. She stalked away, wondering at the anger that flashed through her chest. So he didn't want her healing him. Maybe because he'd seen Billy. Was he disgusted? Others had been. *Why do you do this, Theo?* one of her ex-boyfriends had asked her, honestly baffled. *Why do you hang out with losers? Why do you spend so much of your time with them? It's not like you ever get a thank-you. It's like you don't even notice normal people because they don't need you.*

*I go where I'm called*, Theo thought bitterly, trudging up the stairs. *I do what I'm told. I'm trying to make this world a better place.*

Elise had turned the main lights off. The shop was sunk in shadow, lit only by the few night-lights Theo had installed. She barely noticed, heading for the small kitchen in back, when she heard…What was it? It sounded like a scratching on the glass window that took up the front of the store. She stopped, cocked her head and listened. She was about to continue on when she heard it again.

*Skritch-skritch. Skritch. Scratch-skritch.*

Theo turned, tucking a strand of her hair behind her ear. She searched the dark window, only seeing the familiar street beyond. The French restaurant's window across the street glowed golden, and there were circles of light from the streetlights dotting the pavement. A police car rolled slowly past on the street.

A chill touched Theo's back. She walked across the shop, past the door to the basement, and came to a halt in front of the ancient cash register. Now she could see the entire sidewalk in front of the shop. The slim oak sapling that the city had planted two years ago, when the sidewalks had been repaired, stood bare and leafless. There was an empty paper cup rolling on the sidewalk.

The Cauldron was quiet. There was a murmur of voices from the open door leading to the stairs. Theo listened, her ears straining for any other sound. She felt tense and indecisive. Was her imagination playing tricks on her? That was an occupational hazard for a witch.

The sound came again, a little *skritch-skritch,* as if a small animal was scrabbling at the glass with sharp claws.

Theo walked towards the little glassed-in space where Suzanne would sit on some afternoons and read tarot cards. Mari often cast horoscopes there, tapping into her laptop, which was plugged into a laser printer that Theo kept behind the counter when it wasn't in use. Theo walked slowly up to the window, listening intently.

The *skritch-skritch* came again. It was definitely from that corner. Theo reached the small, round table and stopped, looking out at the corner of Bell Street where it met Fourth Avenue. From here you could look down a block and see the Ave, glimmering with lights. People would be walking along the Ave, even in this weather. But here, a block up, there was nobody on the street. Most of the shops were closed, and the restaurants would be closing soon.

Theo listened, cocking her head, her breathing almost stopped. The chills were coming with intense frequency now, running up her back and her arms and spilling down her legs so that she was shivering. Her teeth wanted to chatter, but she put her tongue in her cheek, stopping them. *What's making that noise?* she thought, and closed her eyes to hear it better.

There was a long moment of silence, and Theo waited. Then the sound came again, a scrabble against the glass, as if it was right in front of her. Right exactly in front of her.

Theo opened her eyes just as a sudden impact spider-webbed the glass window in long silver cracks. She let out a short yell, stumbling back, her arms thrown forward. The Power that had been throbbing in her hands, ready to heal Dante, bulleted forward to meet the glass as well.

The thing hanging in the air, plastered to the window, screamed—a nasty shrill sound that drove right through Theo's head. She fell, banging her already-abused left hip on the floor.

It looked as if it was made out of black smoke. Four red, bulbous, faceted insect eyes were above a wide lipless mouth full of sharp, glassy-black teeth. At least ten legs scrabbled at the glass that was now glowing with the Power Theo had cast at it, holding together the damaged glass.

The wards on the shop glimmered, shivered...and held. They weren't made to take this kind of beating. They were made to keep out shoplifters and robbers. Nothing like this had ever happened before. Theo had always escaped danger by leaving before danger found her.

The thing screamed again, a hot needling sound of agony and lust and hunger. Theo scrabbled backwards, unaware that she was screaming as well, her eyes watering furiously and the Power thundering through her, burning inside her head. She felt it, a physical heat against her cheeks and lips and brain, pressing out through her eyes and tearing at the fabric of her mind. It wanted to *eat* her, she realized. It was *hungry*, and something in Theo would feed it.

Something streaked past her and hit the window from the inside, shattering it. The wards reverberated, and Theo felt an almost physical *snap* as the thing was driven away from the shop. There was a glass-edged snarling going on, up and up to a falsetto squeal that made the other glass windows shiver in their casings. Dante hit the thing squarely. He was shouting, and he had a knife in either hand. The knives seemed to glow red with fury, a crimson light that hurt Theo's eyes.

The blond man had her shoulders, shaking her. "Are you hit?" he yelled over the noise of breaking glass. "*Are you hurt?*"

"N-n-n—" Theo's teeth were chattering too hard for her to speak. She shook her head, mute with shock, and felt a thin trickle of something warm on her upper lip.

"*Fuck!*" The blond man hauled her up as if she weighed nothing and pushed her towards the stairs. His face contorted. Of course. Something about her must hurt him. He had avoided coming close to her. "Get down! Move, woman!" He turned and followed Dante out the broken window, leaping with preternatural speed.

They weren't human. They *couldn't* be human and move like that. Like lightning.

She stumbled for the stairs. When he let her go, her legs wouldn't carry her, and she fell again, rolling over to look back at the broken window. Cold night air poured in, ruffling the racks of cloaks and ritual robes. Glass lay glittering against the wooden floor. Theo rolled onto her side and curled up into a little ball, ignoring the pain in her left hip. If the thing came back through the window, she had to protect the others.

She lay there for what seemed an eternity, feeling the cold floor and the night wind on her cheek. Then, finally, she heard footsteps and broken glass crunching. "Clean that up, can you?" It was Dante. He sounded tired, but the growl in his voice made the entire shop vibrate. "If you're not drained."

"I'm okay, but you'd better look after your witch." The blond man sounded tired too. "She's bleeding. Be careful." He coughed, rackingly, and Theo felt the shop shiver around her. Then the wards settled back into place, humming.

"I always am. I think I almost dislocated my shoulder. Again."

"Serves you right, charging like that. Look at this mess." There was a low thrumming sound. The wards on the shop shifting uneasily, and then the cold air stopped.

Theo opened her eyes to see the blond man patting glass into place on the broken window. The glass was flowing up from the floor and reassembling itself, the cracks healing as if they had never been. She let out a small breath of wonder, and then Dante knelt next to her.

"Oh, no," he said, sliding his arm under her and helping her sit. "Theo? Talk to me." His voice was cracked and hoarse and desperate.

"I heard a...a scratching," she heard herself say, in a small, dazed voice. "I wondered what it was."

"Just a Slider, Theo. They're nocturnal and probably drawn here because of the fight. They're opportunists and pretty easy to kill. They're part of what I'm supposed to defend you against. You're bleeding. I'm so sorry—" His voice was dropping into its lowest registers, and the floor was groaning.

"Calm down," Theo heard herself say. "You'll hurt the shop." Her voice was still small and dreamy, the voice of a woman lost in a concussion. "I think I'm concussed," she said, and her eyes fell closed.

"Theo!" He didn't shake her, but the note of panic in his voice brought her back. "No, don't do that. Stay awake. Stay with me."

"What happened?" Elise's voice was frantic. "Oh my God! What did you do to her? Theo!"

"Elise," Theo sighed, and felt the Elise's warm hands on her skin. A rush of something crimson and scalding roared through her, making Theo gasp and her eyes water with tears again. Elise never did anything halfway.

"Get back," Dante growled. "Get down, you silly witch. There may be more of them."

"Then that's *your* problem," Elise retorted. "Aren't you supposed to keep them off? What did you *do* to her?"

"I didn't...I never should have let her..."

Theo opened her eyes. She looked up at Dante. Something warm and wet dripped into her eyes—blood from a fresh cut on his cheek, slanting up and narrowly missing his left eye. "Oh, my," she said.

"Broken glass," he said very quietly. "It will mend. I'm sorry, Theo. I should have—"

"Can you help me stand up?" she asked. "And we both need that first-aid kit." Her hands were shaking just a little. The Power Elise had poured into her snapped, crackled, made a shower of sparks fall to the ground. There was the smell of candle smoke in the air. "Elise," she said, firmly, "it's all right. I'm all right. Get the tea, please. Dante..."

"The tea," Elise said, standing up, her hands on her hips

and her emerald-green eyes blazing. "You nearly get *killed,* and you're asking me for the *tea.* You really do take the goddamn cake, Theo. You *scared* me."

"Sorry," Theo said, trying to blink. Her eyelashes were sticky with Dante's blood. "I didn't mean to."

"Oh, shut up. Get her downstairs, you...you..." Elise was so furious that she was at a loss for words, something that didn't happen often. Usually she just seemed to stay at a steady pitch of irritation. The smell of burning in the air intensified. "Honestly!" she hissed. "You'd better have a good story for this, *Mister* Dante," she continued, turning on her heel and stalking away. "Tea! Theodora Morgan, you and your...What a perfect pair. Tea! *Tea,* for God's sake—" Her voice faded into furious mumbling as she ducked into the small kitchen. The pale blond man drifted silently after her, exchanging a glance with Dante. He looked even more rumpled and bloody, if that was possible.

"You're bleeding," Dante said. "I'm stupid, Theo. I'm sorry—"

"It's all right," Theo said. Her hip hurt, and she felt her legs turning to rubber. He smelled like gunpowder and rage now, a peppery adrenaline musk that should have been frightening but was instead oddly comforting. "Are you all right?" The comfort made her a little sleepy, and she sighed, leaning into him.

"I'll be fine, if my heart doesn't stop," he said shortly. "Let's get you downstairs and patch you up."

"I'm fine," she said. "Really. Just a bit shaky."

He held her shoulders, helping her to her feet, and steadied her as she almost fell over again. "Dante," she said, remembering his name again, and he froze, looking at her.

Theo leaned forward. Bracing herself on her tiptoes, she kissed his bloody cheek. "You saved my life," she said. "Thank you."

He mumbled something that might have been "you're welcome" and hurried her towards the stairs.

# Sixteen

Dante watched as Suzanne sponged the blood away and examined her. "You've got a nosebleed," the older woman said. "Are you dizzy?"

"Only a little," Theo whispered. Her chestnut hair was tangled, falling over her face and shoulders. Dante's blood had striped her face. Her own blood was merely a little trickle from one nostril.

Strangely enough, it was that one little trickle that disturbed Dante more than his own almost-dislocated shoulder or his bruised ribs—or the cut on his face. The Slider had almost ripped his eye out. When they got desperate, they were tricky.

Hanson was bandaging himself, and the blonde, blue-eyed witch—Mari—was watching. "Does it hurt?' she asked him, and he shrugged, wincing as he dabbed at his shoulder with the peroxide-soaked gauze.

"I heal quickly," he said. "Good thing about being a Watcher. The Dark helps us heal."

"Are there other good things?" Mari asked, her eyes on the gouge. Hanson had been clipped by a levin bolt. The skin looked a little blistered, but it was already starting to pinken and heal. It was disturbing to see for the first time. Dante hoped that the witches wouldn't be any more disturbed than they already were. His stomach was churning with sick fear. Theo had been so close—just one thin piece of glass and the wards between her and a carrion-smelling piece of the Dark.

"I didn't used to think so," Hanson said, and glanced up at her face. She blew a golden curl back out of her eyes, and Hanson smiled, his own eyes a little softer than Dante had ever seen them. The blonde seemed not to notice, her worried eyes on the wound instead of Hanson's face. She missed his crooked smile and the slight movement he made, subtly leaning towards her.

*Well, what do you know,* he thought, shifting a little to ease the pain of his own shoulder. His entire body ached.

*Miracles do happen.*

Theo was looking at him when he turned back from Hanson. Her dark eyes were lit from within, and he blinked. Suzanne finished wiping the blood away, and then she cupped Theo's face in her dry hands. "Theo?" she asked, looking at the younger woman's face.

Theo looked back at the Teacher, blinking. "I'm all right," she said, and she sounded like herself again. "I was just stunned, I think. It was awful."

Elise, her fiery hair pulled back severely, stood by the door to the stairs with her arms crossed over her breasts. "Can we get everyone bandaged up so we can find out what the *hell* is going on here?" she asked, pleasantly. "My patience is really starting to wear thin."

Dante nodded. Now that he was sure Theo was going to be all right, he crossed to the bowl of water Mari had brought and dipped a dark rag in it, wrung it out, and then started to wash off his face. "Where should I start?" he asked nobody in particular. "Hanson and I are Watchers. We're part of the combat arm of Circle Lightfall."

"Combat arm? What the *hell* is Circle Lightfall?" Elise asked.

"A collection of Lightbringers, like yourselves," Hanson said quietly. "Used to be called just the Circle. They started in 1532 in France, a response to the Inquisition. Innocent VIII gave his blessing to the *Malleus Malleficarium.*"

"Kramer and Sprenger." Mari shuddered, and Hanson looked up at her. "Hammer of the Witches."

"Yeah," Hanson said. "They published that and started the witch-hunts. The Catholic Church was losing its grip on the people, and there was a pagan revival of sorts going on. So the church took the easy way out—burn the witches. Trouble is, the movement caught fire in a woman-hating priesthood, and it turned into genocide." He let out a hiss between clenched teeth as he finished dabbing at the wound on his shoulder. His long coat lay to one side, weapons piled on it. "Hand me another gauze, will you?"

Mari did. Their fingers brushed, and Hanson's eyes closed

briefly, reopened.

Dante took up the story. "A cardinal in Innocent's inner circle came up with a great idea. He had been digging in the Vatican Library and came up with some texts—the forbidden kind. He found a way to create the perfect warriors for God. Strong, quick, demonic...and brainless."

Theo was suddenly beside him. "Here," she said, and picked up some gauze and the bottle of peroxide. "Let me."

He nodded and winced as the movement made his shoulder twinge. "So this cardinal—Givelli, called the Gray Demon— brought his idea to the pope. A military order of Masters with brainless zombie Knights, dead men raised from the cemeteries—suicides, men buried in unhallowed ground, criminals." Dante found his eyes locked with Theo's. "And they had these Knights and their hell-dogs—the Seekers, one of which you just saw—hunting down suspected witches. Then the Church found out that the Seekers could see...well, Lightbringers. The ones that shine."

Theo pressed the gauze to the long slice on his cheek, and he inhaled sharply, grateful for the pain. *I might fall into her eyes and never come back,* he thought. *I wouldn't mind that.* "And those ones were almost always village wise women, healers, witches—the ones that the Church had to break if they were to retain temporal power."

Theo's fingers had touched his cheek, and the spike of sensation that caused—the Darkness inside him reacting to the light in her—temporarily blinded him. He inadvertently hissed again. It wasn't pain.

That was enough to startle him. It wasn't pain when she touched him. For the first time, it was pure narcotic pleasure. Every other Lightbringer he'd met had caused a sort of furious agony, the Darkness inside him struggling to escape. But *her* touch soothed him, was a balm to his raw nerves and sore shoulder.

"I'm sorry," Theo said.

"It's all right," he said. *If you touched me again, I wouldn't mind. Even if it hurt, I'd want you to touch me.*

He opened his eyes and found her looking at him, her large

eyes sad and her pretty mouth turned down. "The Circle was formed, Lightbringers banding together to try and escape the Church. Things were bad. Women were being burned at the stake, and Lightbringers were dying everywhere at the hands of the Knights, Gideon de Hauteville, a knight of the Hauteville family, was rescued from death during a battle by a Lightbringer named Jeanne Tourenay. She was a healer, and as soon as Gideon could walk again, he married her. What he didn't know was that she was a part of the Circle, and when the Crusade came to town to find her, he fought them. At some point, something very strange happened."

Theo sponged the blood off his forehead and cleaned the slice along his hairline. "What happened?" she asked. Dante had forgotten there were other people in the room. He had, in fact, even forgotten what he was saying. He simply looked at her face. Silence stretched between them, a silence that dipped Dante's body in honey. He swallowed harshly, trying to keep control.

"Well, the records are confused," Hanson said. His shoulder was bandaged now, and he held up his coat. His bare skin was glimmering pale in the candlelight. "Our oral tradition says that Gideon struck a bargain with something, but we don't know what it was. The upshot is, he was given three gifts. The first was speed and strength to overpower the Seekers and the Knights. The second gift he was given was a black knife with runes worked into the blade and hilt, and the secret of how to make other rune-knives. Damn. Another bit of sewing I have to do." He sounded mournful as he eyed his coat.

"Here," Mari said. "Hand it over, I'll see what I can do." She sounded very matter-of-fact, businesslike.

Hanson complied. Dante looked back at Theo, who was biting her lower lip as she cleaned the cut on his scalp. He found that completely charming—and completely distracting. What had he been saying?

"What was the third gift?" the redhead, Elise, asked from the door.

"The third gift was his bond with Jeanne," Dante answered. "She was his witch, after all. It gave him the chance to defend her effectively against the Crusade. That's the lure held out for Watchers, you know. The chance that we might find a witch to bond with, a Lightbringer that we can...Well, you understand," he finished lamely. Theo was applying some sort of herbal paste to the cut at his hairline. She was careful not to touch her bare skin to his. But she was leaning close, her hair falling forward. Even tangled and mussed, it was gorgeous. He drew in a long breath, filling his lungs with the smell of her hair. He could track her anywhere now.

"No," Elise said. "I don't understand. What if this witch doesn't want anything to do with your Circle, or with your Crusade, or with your Watchers?"

"Then the Watcher withdraws," Hanson said. "And he just watches. If the Crusade moves in, he takes care of the Lightbringer as best he can. Dante's brought five Lightbringers into Circle Lightfall so far, but none of them have been *his* witch. We're not here to push, fire-witch. We're here to help."

"It's not just the Crusade," Dante said. "They pursue Lightbringers where they can, but they're dying out. The biggest dangers nowadays are the stray bits of Darkness—the predators and carrion-eaters, like the Slider that just attacked. Lightbringers attract Darkness. I'm sure you have all been attacked, one way or another, without realizing it. But you're working together now, and you're more powerful than ever. As a result, more of the Dark is attracted to you. The more powerful you are as Lightbringers, the more vulnerable you are. It's the price you pay."

"This is the biggest crock of—" the redhead began.

"Elise," Theo said softly, and Elise stopped short. "Whatever I saw outside the store was *evil*," she continued, still applying that paste to his head. It smelled awful, but he could tell that she had made it. It was already helping the wound to heal. She had such incredible power.

"Or if not evil, then at least very dangerous," she went on. "If it could have come through the glass and the wards we've put on the store, I think it would have killed me." She was studying her work with great concentration, her fingers butterfly-light. "And this man dove right through the window without even pausing," she continued. "He saved my life, with no thought for his own. We at least owe him some courtesy."

"He just walks in here with *guns* and you—" Elise began again.

"Yes," Theo said. "I'm doing it again, aren't I? Another one of my strays. One of these days I'll trust the wrong person and end up dead. Can we move on to a different argument now?" Her voice held a little sharpness, and she looked down into Dante's face. "I know that these things hunt...I've felt them before. That's why I've moved around all my life, ever since my parents died."

"You won't end up dead," he said. "Not if I can help it."

"This is all very well," Suzanne said. "But what does this Circle Lightfall want from us?"

Dante sighed. It was a good question. "If you like, you can join them and add your power to the Lightbringers we have already. They're trying to turn back the tide."

"What tide?" Mari asked. "There." She looked at the muscle flickering under Hanson's skin and seemed to blush. She was doing something with his coat, her long fingers glowing softly with Power. "A minor mending, but it should hold. Easier just to do it with needle and thread, but I need the practice." She smiled shyly at Hanson, who grinned back. "Suzanne's always after me to practice."

"My thanks, Lightbringer," Hanson said. "The tide—the Circle's noticed that when there are a certain number of Lightbringers in a city, the crime rate goes down. So does the suicide rate, and the domestic violence rate. People start acting nicer. The Circle thinks that if we can get enough Lightbringers in the world—and stop the Crusade and the Dark hunting them—it will be like the old hundredth-monkey thing. If not world peace, then at least a hell of a lot closer."

"Then why wasn't it more peaceful before the Inquisition?" the redhead asked. She didn't look mollified in the least. As a matter of fact, she looked more suspicious.

Hanson sighed. "I don't know. It's just theory."

Theo leaned back. "There," she said. "And your shoulder...What should we do with that? Some arnica, maybe?" Her tangled hair fell forward, and she shoved it back again. Dante twitched, wanting to brush at her hair, stopping himself.

"I'll be all right," Dante said. He forced himself to continue with the story. "One of the theories is that Lightbringers were scarce even before the inquisition because of the female infanticide rate in the ancient world. And there was a time when there were a lot of Lightbringers, before Atlantis disappeared in the cataclysm. Atlantis was the last great Lightbringer civilization. We think that we can create another one. A world without war, or poverty, or hatred—that's what Circle Lightfall wants. Or at least a world with much less war and hatred."

"I'm exceedingly wary of utopias," the Teacher muttered, her sharp face pursed into lines of disapproval. "I think we should all go home and think this over. Theo?"

"I guess so," Theo replied. She retreated from Dante and picked up a green-painted tea mug. "I have to open the shop tomorrow. And there're my rounds to make."

"Dante." Hanson was now looking at him. He tore his eyes away from Theo's profile and found the other Watcher looking critically at him. "We have three Lightbringers, a Teacher, and only two Watchers. How are we going to swing this?"

"Excuse me," Elise said, politely. Her pretty porcelain face was set and angry. "If I understand you right, you're thinking you can boss us around in the name of self-defense. I can take care of myself, thank you. I'll meet you here tomorrow, Theo."

Theo's forehead creased. "Elise—" she began. "Shouldn't we listen to them? I have to admit, I'm more than halfway convinced. You didn't *see* that thing. It was awful." She shuddered and cupped her elbows in her hands, hugging herself, Dante's jaw set.

"How do we know *they* didn't bring it?" Elise asked. "Huh? How do we know?"

Dante looked over at her, his mouth turning back into a straight line. "I'll forgive you that, because you don't know us," he said, softly. "Do you honestly think that I'd let *anything* harm her—or that I'd bring anything evil into her vicinity?"

Elise stared back at him. Her face lost a little bit of its sharpness. "Maybe not," she said. "I think you might actually be serious."

The air stirred uneasily inside the little temple. Suzanne clapped her hands, sharply. "Let's not be idiots," she said crisply. "I brought the van. I'll drive everyone home, and come and pick Elise up tomorrow afternoon. I think it makes sense to be as cautious as possible, don't you, Elise?"

Now the fire-haired witch shrugged. "I guess so," she admitted grudgingly. "I suppose we'd better clean up, then. This is a mess."

"It certainly is," Hanson agreed, shrugging back into his bloody T-shirt. "I'm going to have to call in and get reinforcements."

"If there are any to spare," Dante said, rising to his feet. He gave his leather coat a shake, to make sure it fell the way he wanted it to. His shoulder gave one last twinge and subsided, healing rapidly. The pain was going away. As long as he stayed near Theo and kept his cool, he wouldn't feel it. Much. He would feel that excruciating pleasure instead. "I'll help clean up. Theo, you just rest, okay?"

"No thanks," she said, smiling at him. Her beautiful dark-green eyes now had huge circles under them. "That's one of the rules—everyone helps clean around here." She bent down, picked up a stack of plates. "We'll save the leftovers for tomorrow," she said. "Suzanne, you want to go warm up the van? It's cold out there."

"I'll cover her," Hanson said, shrugging into his coat. "Thanks, Mari. It's a good patch." He was making his weapons disappear into the coat's darkness, his sword already strapped on against the dark leather.

"You're welcome," she said, blushing furiously. She started to repack the first-aid kit, dropping the bottle of peroxide and then spilling the gauze packets. "Oh, no."

"Oh, for the love of—" Elise stalked away from the door and knelt down to help Mari. "Honestly. Am I the only one around here who hasn't lost her mind?"

"Maybe," Theo said, smiling. Suzanne touched her shoulder. The older woman was smiling too, but only faintly.

"I'll warm up the van," she said.

"Good." Theo looked over at Dante. "Can you help me pick these up?"

He made sure his guns were riding as they should be and his knives were in place. Then he looked at her, tired and disheveled and absolutely beautiful. "Sure," he said.

*I am in so much trouble,* he thought, and bent down to start collecting takeout cartons.

# Seventeen

Suzanne's van was a big purple monstrosity, surprisingly comfortable even with all six of them in it. She dropped Elise off first, and Hanson walked her up to her door. She lived in a little duplex on Fourth Street, a block from the store. Mari was next—she lived near Theo, renting a room in a house full of college students. Hanson, visibly torn, finally got out of the van with her when Suzanne informed him that she could take care of herself, and that she didn't want him knowing where she lived. "I don't trust you," she said, coolly, "and if I'm attacked, I'm capable of defending myself. Good night, young man. You keep Mari safe, or I'll deal with you."

"Come on," Mari said. "I'll wash your shirt."

And that was that. Theo smiled to see shy little Mari leading the tall man as if he was a puppy. He went along docilely. If Theo's guesses were right, the man wouldn't know what hit him. Mari was only shy and quiet until she figured out what she wanted—just like a python. Looked like she had a new conquest.

Then it occurred to Theo that she didn't know anything about these men, and she glanced over at Suzanne, whose sharp hazel eyes hadn't missed a single thing. "It's all right, Theo," Suzanne said shortly. "Remember the cards?"

Theo shivered. *Knight of Swords. Three of Swords. The Tower. Three of Cups. Queen of Pentacles.* "What did you get from that?" she asked the older woman, almost forgetting that Dante was in the middle seat behind the driver's seat. Theo herself rode shotgun, as usual. Suzanne often counted on her to navigate. She frequently said that Elise was such a horrible back seat driver that she belonged in the trunk, and that Mari, with her horror of traffic, was just as bad. "I just remember you saying something about the Knight of Swords meaning a load of trouble, and the Tower meaning great change. The Three of cups—that's us, but who's missing?"

"You weren't listening." Suzanne sniffed, shifted into

"drive" and pulled away from the curb. "Your friend here is the Knight of Swords. I would have thought *that* was obvious to you. You're being called upon to make a choice, Theo, like I've always said. You've put it off for years."

"Just because I don't want to be—" Theo began, and then remembered Dante. She looked back at him, but he appeared to be asleep. Theo had no idea how he could sleep with the sword strapped to his back.

It had been a long day, and she was exhausted. "I don't want to fight with you, Suzanne," she said, softly. "I didn't sleep well last night, and today…I could have done without this."

Suzanne snorted. "Should have thought of that before you incarnated as a witch, then. And a witch of rare power, too. You are meant for more than this, Theo. You have work to do," she said. Her long silver hair was falling out of its coronet, and she looked tired too. The cheerful yellow of her poncho helped a little, but it was dark, and late—eleven p.m. according to the dashboard clock. "It's all right, dear. I keep telling you, we're in Her hands."

"What do you know about these people?" Theo asked softly.

"Not enough," Suzanne replied. "I'll do some research tonight. But I don't think he'll hurt you. He seems…" Suzanne's hazel eyes slid up to the rearview mirror. "He's watching you."

Theo turned to look. Dante's eyes were open, glittering in the darkness. "Are you hurting?" she asked him.

"Not particularly," he said. "Just checking."

Theo turned back to the front window. She watched the pavement slip smoothly by under the van's wheels. "I wonder how Billy's doing," she said, quietly. "It's cold out tonight."

"You can't save everyone," Suzanne said. This was an old conversation, comforting in its familiarity.

"I know," Theo said. "That doesn't make it any easier. He was so thin, Suzanne. He had sores up and down his arms."

"It's not your fault," Suzanne replied, taking a right turn on Willow Street. "You didn't shove the needle in his arm. Nor did you give him the drugs."

"But he keeps going back to it…" Theo sighed.

"Why don't you talk about what's really bothering you?" Suzanne's eyes were focused on the road.

"That awful thing wanted to kill me," Theo whispered, and shuddered. "What's happening, Suzanne? What's happening to me?"

"Nothing but fate coming home to roost," the older woman said practically. "We've been waiting for this storm ever since you opened that store and hired Elise and Mari on the same day. We knew you were the one. And you've been running from the Dark all your life. When are you going to stop running?"

Theo blew out a long sigh. The van was warm, and she felt oddly safe. The vision of red bug-eyes and scrabbling legs going *skritch-skritch* on the glass faded. "You sound so calm," she said. "I wish I was."

"Your time is coming, Theo," Suzanne said, and then braked to a stop in front of Theo's house. "All right, kids, everyone out of the pool. I'm going home to soak my feet." She sounded tired.

"Promises, promises." Theo laughed, and then leaned over to kiss the older woman's cheek. "I love you, Suzanne. See you tomorrow."

"Thank you, Teacher," Dante said gravely, reaching for the side door handle. He opened the door and got out, managing to look everywhere at once. He closed the door and stood waiting.

"Do you trust him?" Theo asked.

Suzanne glanced at her. "Maybe. He's the Knight of Swords. A good ally," she said, slowly. "Go on now. Get inside, and be careful."

Theo nodded, biting her lip, and Dante opened her door. She slid out of the van and stood on the sidewalk, watching Suzanne drive slowly away. The air was chill and still, clouds covering the night sky and hiding the moon. Dante stood next to her, not hurrying her, just waiting.

Finally, Theo saw Suzanne's brake lights vanish around the corner. She lived on Rambaugh Street, five blocks up from

Willow. She turned to the tall man who had dived through a pane of cracked glass at something very much like a nightmare with red eyes. And she had never seen him before last night…

"You saved my life," she said, awkwardly.

He shrugged, his coat moving on his shoulders. "You're cold," he said. "You should go inside."

"Do you have anywhere to go?" she asked him.

"Circle Lightfall rented me a room near here. It's okay, Theo. I won't push you."

Theo shivered and looked up to find his black eyes fixed on her. His face, marred by the scratches, was still handsome in a cold, severe way. She swallowed, suddenly aware that he had been looking at her all evening, whenever he hadn't actually been fighting or answering someone else's questions. He'd been staring at her. It was unsettling, to be watched so closely.

She was tired, cold, and hungry again. "Why don't you come in?" she said. "Please. It's the least I can do. And I want you to explain this to me."

He nodded. "If you like," he said, quietly. "Are you sure you want to invite me in?"

She examined him, from his spiky hair to his black boots. "Why not?" she said, and couldn't seem to wipe the smile off her face. "You did save my life, and you seem like a nice guy." She shivered, hugging herself through her pea coat. "And you watched me heal Billy and didn't try to stop me."

He shrugged. "You should go inside," he said.

"Right." Theo cocked her head. Her hair was tangled and dirty, and her hip hurt, and her head was beginning to ache, too. "You mean you won't come in?"

He finally smiled, looking down at her. "No, I didn't say that at all."

# Eighteen

She left him standing in the living room and told him to make himself at home. Then she disappeared upstairs to take a shower. Dante walked from room to room, his hands stuffed in his pockets. The urge to touch something of hers was overwhelming, so he fought it.

There were shelves of books, green glass bottles in all shades, a green wall hanging—a tapestry of jungle leaves— and plants everywhere. Ferns and philodendrons hung from hooks in the ceiling. Swedish ivy was set in terra-cotta pots on the bookshelves. African violets and spider plants. Something that looked suspiciously like an orange tree grew in a huge green pot by a south-facing window. Rubber trees, a lemon eucalyptus, coleus, orchids—he gave up trying to identify the different plants. This witch's affinity was plain.

There was a fat, sleek black cat sleeping on the couch, and it opened one yellow eye to measure him. Then, apparently judging him no threat, it went back to sleep. He saw the subtle shimmer of a warding in the air around the cat, Theo's light touch and green-tinted Power evident.

She had hung three glass fishing-floats in the eastern window, and the pendants from crystal chandeliers in the south windows. All in all the house was crowded, a little dusty, and smelled like green things and the dry scent of book pages, with the odor of some sweet incense mixed in.

He liked it, liked the plants and the Egyptian touches— little blue scarab beads, a statue of Hathor, another of Anubis, carved from obsidian. There was a rough rock statue of Sekhmet, and a statue of Artemis as well. So she was an eclectic, this witch. There was another small statue of Hotei, the Laughing Buddha.

It was an odd feeling to be inside her house. He had walked past it last night, and imagined what it would be like. He had imagined silks, velvets, lots of light. Books, certainly— Lightbringers loved books. And little bits of curious things, for amulets and decorations. There was no television. That was a little surprising. A stack of CDs by a small stereo turned out to be jazz and classical. She apparently liked Sinatra too. Good, a woman with taste.

There was a fireplace with an altar set on the hearthstone, an athame lying across a piece of fine linen that had a rune for health embroidered on it. It rang with calm power. So she was working on a healing spell for someone.

*I found out what I was from books,* her voice said, cool and calm inside his head. *I've always known I was different.*

What had it been like for her? Parents dead in an auto accident, and her moving from place to place, living by her wits. Why had she settled here? Probably tired of running. She had acquired the Cauldron and was doing well, from the looks of it. It was probably the first time in her life she had possessed everything she needed. She would be reluctant to give it up and flee the Dark again.

He was examining a black and white print—a photograph of a bunch of glass marbles lying on a piece of crushed velvet— when she came down the stairs and stepped into the living room, wearing a pretty dark-green silk nightgown. Long sleeves belled over her hands, and the skirt brushed her feet. "One of my friends did that," she said, smiling at him. Her long hair was braided back, simply, and her cheeks were flushed from the heat of the shower. "Lenny King. Isn't it great?"

He nodded, the words drying up in his throat. Her neck was a little damp, the water gleaming on her skin, and she smelled like sandalwood soap and dampness. Dante was suddenly very aware that he hadn't had a shower in two days, that he had dried blood in his hair, and that he was only a weapon. Nothing very special at all, just a weapon.

She stood in the door of the room in blithe disregard of any danger, her attention on the print hanging on the wall next to him. Suddenly, he saw himself, his long black coat and his weapons, just a blot of bloody Darkness in the beauty that she had created.

She came across the room on bare feet, swaying, the skirt of her nightgown making that low sound that only silk could make. He watched her face—a long nose and a beautiful mouth, her eyes large and liquid, her hair pulled back. The brightness of her eyes, the charcoal fan of her eyelashes, and the vulnerable little notch between her collarbones. The shape of her breasts under the silk. The way she moved, like liquid power.

He had almost touched her shoulder before he remembered and pulled his hand back. She looked up at him. "Why don't you take a shower?" she asked, kindly. "And I'll wash your clothes. I've got a pair of sweatpants that might fit you—old ex-boyfriend. He wasn't as tall as you, but he liked his pants a little loose," she grimaced, her mobile mouth turning down. "A little too loose," she continued. "He ended up cheating on me with some bar floozy. Thought I wouldn't know. Sometimes it's a bitch being psychic."

"I guess," he said, his throat almost stoppered with the things he wanted to say. Who would ever want to leave a house that she was in? Who would not count himself lucky to be in her presence? Who—

*Oh, ouch,* he thought, grimly. *This is going to hurt. I am in so much trouble.*

She blinked, maybe not understanding him, and smiled. It was a glorious smile. "Are you psychic?" she asked him. "You seem to have some Power."

"Only in a limited way," he answered, automatically. "Mostly thanks to the training."

"What kind of training?" she asked. "No, wait. Go take a shower. I've left the sweatpants up there for you, and a towel, too. Bring your clothes down. I've got a load of wash to do. I'm hungry. Are you hungry?" She took a deep breath. "The problem with Chinese is that it fills you up, and then you're hungry an hour later. What about a beer? Do you like beer?"

He shook his head. "Don't drink. Don't smoke, either." He watched the flush rise in her cheeks.

"I suppose that's good," she said. "I'm babbling. I know I'm babbling. Go take a shower, will you? I'll cook something."

He nodded. *Gods,* he thought, *I'm acting stupid. She's uncomfortable with me here, and all I can do is stand here like a big dumb Watcher. All muscle, no brain—*"I'm going," he said. "If anything's wrong, I'll feel it and come down."

She bit her lip, a shadow crossing her face, and Dante felt his heart fall inside his chest. "Look," he continued, "it's going to be okay, all right? I promise. Nothing's going to happen tonight. Thank you for your kindness."

Theo nodded. "I'll just go start making us something to eat," she said, and backed away, almost tripping over a pillow lying on the floor. Then she whirled and vanished into the kitchen. Dante tried not to smile. Something crashed in the kitchen, and he heard her curse with an inventiveness that raised his eyebrows. Then she started to hum, the same song she had been singing last night, and that reminded him of why he was here.

*She's my witch,* he thought, with a kind of amazement. *It's happened. It's finally happened.* He looked down at his callused hands, scarred from practice and combat, wide fingers and thick bones. Then he shook himself and started upstairs to wash the blood and stink of Dark off.

*Now all I have to do is keep her alive.*

# Nineteen

Cooking always helped.

Theo was soon singing out loud while she scrambled eggs and whipped egg whites for waffles. "Bring me down to the god in the glen, bring me down to the green trees dancing. Bring me down to the Lady's mirror, bring me down to the place of the dance..." Suzanne's song again. She alternated between singing about Mexico and about the god in the glen, and soon felt much less nervous. Thorin, the cat, began twining around her ankles, and that helped too.

She had found Thorin in a cardboard box, shivering and sick, a year ago on Samhain. She was on her way home from the Halloween party she and Elise had gone to after the magick was done. The cat had been a ball of fur and bones, too sick to protest when Theo picked him up. His soft sounds of distress had brought her into the alley he'd been abandoned in. Now he was sleek and glossy, and as arrogant as any king. She refilled his water dish and was rewarded with a meow of thanks.

She didn't have any bacon, but she did have some tofu sausage, and she was trying to decide whether or not to cook them when Dante ghosted into her green and white kitchen, his black hair wet and slick, wearing a pair of black sweatpants and a ragged black *Kite Fighters* T-shirt. Her song trailed off. Thorin simply looked up from his food dish, slitted his eyes, and went back to eating.

So Dante had Thorin's stamp of approval. Well, he would be the first man who ever had.

The tall man was carrying his dirty clothes, and she pointed at a basket full of laundry set by the basement stairs. He tossed them accurately into the basket. "I had an extra shirt," he said, and Theo almost swallowed her tongue. He had the knives she'd seen before, but there was no sign of the guns. Or the sword.

"Do you carry around extra clothes in that big coat?" she asked, and then looked down at the waffle iron. "Oh, Goddess," she said. "I hope I don't burn these. I'm so tired. I'm sorry, this isn't going to be any good—"

"Is that tofu?" he asked, his eyebrows rising.

Theo tried not to look at how dark his eyes were, and at his shoulders. "I didn't have any bacon," she said.

"Oh," he said. "Vegetarian?"

She nodded, biting at her lower lip so she wouldn't babble at him. It didn't work. *What is wrong with me? I haven't acted like this since high school!*

"I just had to, she said. I couldn't stand the thought of a cow dying…I really couldn't. I went to a slaughterhouse once, to see where meat came from, and I was sick for two weeks."

"No wonder," he said. "A psychic in a slaughterhouse. You must have been horrified."

She was *blushing*, she realized, and dropped the spatula she was holding. It hit the counter and bounced, and his hand shot out and caught it. "I was, actually," she said. "Look, waffles, and scrambled eggs, and those things—if you want them. I want to ask you—" *How did he do that? How does he move so quickly?*

He was leaning against the end of the counter, his arms folded across his chest. She looked at his eyes, and then decided that would get her into trouble and looked at his shoulders. That wasn't any better. Then his chest—*Goddess, does he have to be so big?* she thought, and blushed even more fiercely. "Go ahead," he said. "Ask me anything."

She took the spatula back and noticed that he avoided touching her fingers. "Why won't you let me touch you?" she asked.

He shook his head a little, the corner of his sinful mouth lifting up a little. "Nice and direct," he said. "You know how to ask, don't you?"

Before she realized what she was doing, she grimaced at him and kept stirring the eggs. The waffle iron's light went off, and she flipped it open, revealing a beautifully golden-brown waffle, steaming gently. She flipped it out with practiced skill, added it to a plate that already held another waffle, lifted the egg-pan, and flipped out some of the scrambled eggs.

"There," she said, pleased with herself. "Here, take it." She handed him the plate, and he took it, looking surprised. "There's butter and syrup right there. Speak now, or taste no sausages."

"Do they qualify as sausages?" he asked, a mischievous glint in his black eyes.

"Oh, go sit down," she said, tossing the box of tofu sausages onto the counter. "You're probably a carnivore."

"Mm." He added a little butter to his waffles and doused them in syrup. "I eat what I have to, most of the time. I've eaten some pretty awful things. There was that time in..." He trailed off. "Where should I sit?"

She took a sip of orange juice and waved him towards the living room. Her own plate held scrambled eggs and would soon have a waffle, too. "In there. We can talk and eat like uncivilized people."

"Uncivilized?" he asked. "You strike me as being very civilized." He was smiling slightly, and the hot flush rushed up Theo's cheeks again.

"Why won't you let me touch you?" she asked, taking care not to drop the spatula again.

"I'll go sit down."

He left the room, and Theo had the completely reprehensible urge to throw the spatula after him. Who did he think he was fooling?

*Me,* she thought, *and doing a damn good job of it, too.* "What do you want to drink?" she called after him.

"Water's fine," he said, from the living room. "I can get it."

"Oh, no you don't." Theo finished another waffle, and looked in despair at the batter she'd made. She'd be in here for a half-hour, cooking these. "I'll bring it."

She decided to leave the extra batter in the fridge and carried her plate and his water glass out into the living room. He was actually sitting on the floor, with his back towards the wall next to the fireplace. The only place in the room where he could see all the entrances and exits, including the windows, she realized. He wasn't sitting in any of the chairs because he wanted to be able to see everything. And the black coat, with his sword lying on top of it, was right next to him. Theo swallowed dryly and handed him his water glass. She set her plate down on his other side and went to get her orange juice.

"Now," she said, settling back down, "do you mind answering my question, or are you going to put me off again?"

"This is really good," he said. "I'll answer."

"Good," she said. "Well?"

He took a deep breath and set his plate aside. She noticed that he'd eaten half his waffle and most of the scrambled eggs. "Habit, kind of. It's because I'm a Watcher," he said. "If you accept the responsibility—of being a Watcher—there's a price. And part of that price is that it hurts to be around Lightbringers. Something about the...the Darkness in us. Most of us aren't nice people, and we've got this one last chance to do things right, you know?"

Theo shook her head. Her braid was still wet, and it had made a little damp spot against the small of her back. "You seem nice enough to me," she said shyly, and then she wanted to smack herself. *Did I really just say that? How dumb can I be?*

But he gave her a lopsided angelic smile, and she forgot to breathe. "That's good," he said. "I'd hate to have you afraid of me. It's just that to do what we do we have to be mean. We're a bunch of riffraff."

"Does it hurt you, if I touch you?" She heard the wistful tone in her own voice and took a bite of waffle.

"Not exactly," he said. "You're my witch. I wouldn't call it pain, coming from you. But it's distracting, and it's my habit to avoid touching a Lightbringer."

Theo took this in and decided that a change of subject was probably best. "Well, where do you come from?" she asked him. "It's like pulling teeth, talking to you."

He shrugged. "I've gotten used to not saying much about it. I was in the Marines for a while, in a war zone. That's all I want to say. It was awful. I came home with a case of combat jitters and was halfway to the nuthouse when a Lightbringer— she was a little like you, except she was part of Circle Lightfall and had a Watcher— brought me out of it. It was...it was like wandering around in a haze, just stumbling around with my head stuck on blood and dying and…" He seemed to remember that he was talking to her and looked at her. "She brought me out, and they told me that I could make up for all the things I'd done. That I could be useful. So once I healed up, I took the training and here I am."

Theo found that her appetite had vanished. Thorin came strolling in and stole a bit of scrambled egg from her plate. She petted him without thinking about it, smoothing his fur. "What kind of training?"

"Apprenticed to other Watchers," he said. "It was just like basic training, in a way. Don't move, don't talk, don't even breathe unless the man says it's okay."

"Are there any female Watchers?" she asked. Thorin finished chewing on the scrambled eggs and walked over to Dante. He investigated Dante's knee and then stalked away. He leapt up onto the couch and settled into his habitual ball, closing his eyes.

Dante shook his head, pushing his damp hair back with stiff fingers. It began to stick up in soft little spikes, maybe remembering that he was supposed to be tough. Theo had to hide a smile, but his own mouth turned down at the corners. "How many women do you know who can slit a throat?" he asked. "Or break someone's neck? It takes a lot to push a woman to the point of violence, and, well, we need to be able to go there sooner."

Theo shivered. He said it so calmly it was hard to grasp. It was like the violence didn't even matter to him. It was just something he lived with. "What about Lightbringers?" she asked. "Are any of them male?"

"Some," he admitted. "They get assigned Watchers, too, and sometimes…well, there are a few gay Watchers. They're actually tougher than some of us straight guys." He took another bite of waffle. "They bond just like the rest of us do."

"So…it hurts you to be around me?" she asked, hearing the wistfulness in her voice again.

"It's just distracting," he said. "That'll stop at some point, I guess. It's actually…it feels good to have you touch me.

Almost too good." He was eating quickly, with neat manners, but still making the food vanish. "You're my witch."

Theo took a sip of orange juice. "How do you know?" she asked, fascinated.

"I just do," he said. "I knew the first time I saw you." He stopped eating long enough to look at her, his black eyes focused on her face, and Theo shifted uncomfortably.

"When was that? How long have you been following me around?"

He shifted a little, took a drink of water. "I just got into town last night."

"You followed me home last night?" she asked. *I knew it. I knew it was him. "That's right, go home. You're safe, I promise." That was him. Goddess, that was him!*

"Well, yes, actually. I was laying traps around your block, defenses. There was a Seeker following you last night."

"A Seeker…like the thing at the shop?" Theo's throat was dry. She took another drink of juice.

He nodded. His hair was drying rapidly and beginning to look softer, not slick with water. He ran his hand back through it, obviously used to having it up in gelled spikes, and grimaced a little. "Yeah. The thing at the shop was a Slider, not a Seeker. Sliders work alone, they feed on psychics and addicts. The Seeker following you was the kind that the Crusade uses to kill Lightbringers. Good thing I was there."

Theo realized that she was shaking. She set her orange juice down. "I should go put the laundry in the wash," she said, her voice thin and tight. She made it to her feet in a rush, almost upsetting her glass. He grabbed it, his hand moving so quickly it blurred.

"Theo," he said. "It's okay. You've got time to get used to the idea."

"What idea?" she asked, her voice shaking. "I suppose I have no choice, not if I want to keep living here. This is my home now, and you're telling me that if I stay…those things will keep coming after me. And you…what do you want from me?"

Dante set her glass down carefully. "Nothing you don't

want to give," he said. "I'll wait for you, Theo. I mean it."

"Wait for *what?*" she almost yelled, and then closed her eyes and took a deep breath. The windows were rattling with her anger. Something inside her that had Suzanne's voice was telling her to calm down. She could hurt someone or something if she lost control. Thorin looked up from his perch on the couch. His ears were laid back, and his yellow eyes were slitted.

"Theo," Dante said, softly. Just that.

Theo took a deep breath. "Wait for what?" she repeated, a little more calmly. "What is it that you want from me, Dante?"

"Anything you care to give," he said, and looked down at his plate. "You stop the pain, Theo. I was…Well, I never believed in a lot of what Circle Lightfall says about the Watchers and the Lightbringers, but I think I'm starting to. I think I was meant to be your protection, Theo. If you don't…I mean, if you can't stand the thought of me being with you…"

"No," Theo said. "It's not that. It's just that…I don't even know you."

He looked up at her, his black eyes hot with something she didn't want to name. "Are you sure you don't?" he asked, softly. "Because I feel like I know you."

"I should go do the laundry," Theo said, in a high breathless voice.

"I don't want to scare you," he said, and she could see that he meant it. It was a nice thought, but Theo was already frightened. "Really, Theo. I don't."

"I know you don't," she said. "I just don't like the thought of being forced into a…a relationship, just because I'm afraid."

"I won't force you into anything," he said, shortly. He dropped his eyes. "Go on, then. It's okay." He set his plate aside and dropped his hands onto his knees, in a classic meditation posture. "I'll wait for you, forever if I have to."

*Why does he have to say things like that?* Theo retreated to the kitchen and carried the laundry basket downstairs with shaking hands. Her basement was dark, with boxes stacked neatly on one side, and her laundry room on the other. She stood leaning on the washer, her knees weak and trembling, and then she stuffed the dark clothes into the machine. His shirt had blood on it. She wondered if it was all his.

*How many women do you know who can slit a throat?* His voice had been so even, so matter-of-fact. *It takes a lot to push a woman to the point of violence. They told me that I could make up for all the things I'd done. That I could be useful.*

*I'll wait for you, forever if I have to.*

*You stop the pain.*

*I feel like I know you.*

She dumped some soap into the washer, which was rapidly filling with water. She added the clothes, and the way some of the soapsuds turned pink made her faintly sick.

*I can't do this,* she thought, and closed the washer's lid.

*But he needs healing.* The deep voice that led her from place to place sometimes spoke up inside her head. *Can you say that he doesn't? Perhaps even more than some of the others. And you're a healer, Theo. You go where you're led. Right?*

"I don't want to," she murmured, looking at the washer. It started to chug. "He frightens me."

*He needs healing, Theo,* the deep voice replied. *You go where you're led. Right?*

"Oh, *damn* it," she said, and would have kicked the washer, except that her feet were bare and already chilled from the concrete floor. He'd gone straight out through the shop window at full speed, at the red-eyed thing that had howled at her, scrabbling at the glass and trying to get to her. Putting his body between her and that thing.

*And he is an absolute hunk,* she thought, hearing Mari's voice. *"You're so lonely…"*

"I am standing here talking to myself," she said out loud, looking down at the washer. "While he's upstairs, probably laughing at me. I'm such a ditz. All right, Theodora, what are you going to do? Play it by ear, I suppose. I've never been chased by big black spider thingies with glowing red eyes. And I think he's telling the truth. I think he really means well, but I'm not sure about the rest of this."

She nodded to herself smartly and shivered. "He's probably

wondering what happened to me. Did I get eaten by big, black, red-eyed spiders down here?"

Theodora tried to laugh, but it died on her lips. "I don't know," she said out loud to her boxes. "I think I trust *him*. But what about these Circle Lightfall people? I'm not sure I like what I hear about them. Did he *ask* to be taken into this, or was he just dragged in like me? And I did ask for some excitement...Goddess, I forgot those terms and conditions again...The Knight of Swords..."

"I do feel like I know him," she continued, whispering under the sound of the washer. "That's part of the problem. I've never...I mean, I always...Oh, *damn* it..."

"Theo?" Dante's voice. It sounded like he was at the head of the stairs. "Are you all right?"

"Fine," she called, and started towards the stairs. *As fine as I can be. I should know better than to ask for a man. Look at what happens. A total hunk gets dumped in my lap. A total hunk wearing guns and talking about slitting throats and waiting for me forever and a circle of Lightbringers. Lucky me.* "Go get some more to eat."

"I'm done. Are you okay?"

"Just woolgathering, I suppose." Theo reached the bottom of the stairs and looked up. Dante stood at the top of the stairs, silhouetted against the light from the kitchen. He looked tall, and just as dangerous, but he also looked...Well, a little...

Lonely.

*Oh, Goddess.* Theo thought. *There goes my heart.* "I think I should go to bed," she managed to say. "I'm beginning to feel a little..."

"It's hard to take, at first," he said. "I'll sleep on the couch, if that's okay with you."

The sheer lunacy of the situation rose up and made Theo laugh. He was standing there in his black T-shirt and her ex-boyfriend's sweatpants, the knives strapped to his torso. His hair was mussed, and the cuts on his face were almost closed now. He was healing quickly. Maybe it was from being around her...and maybe not. And he had just offered to sleep on the couch, like a perfect gentleman.

Did he have to be a gentleman too?

Theo climbed the stairs slowly, feeling the cold slick wood against her feet. When she got to the top, he stepped back, slowly, as if he wanted to touch her. He had dark circles under his black eyes, and he looked about as tired as Theo actually felt. "Sure," she said, finally. "That's okay. Blankets are in the hall closet."

"I can find them," he said. "You go up to bed. Sleep well. I'll be here."

She nodded and slid past him. He didn't move. "Turn the lights out when you go to bed," she said, and heard him let out a deep, frustrated sigh. "Good night, Dante. I think I can trust you. I hope I'm right."

"You can," he said. "Good night, Theo. Sleep well."

# Twenty

The phone rang.

Dante sat up, blinking. He'd slept deeply for perhaps the first time in five years, and his mouth felt a little sandy. There had been no attack, not even a ripple against the traps he'd set.

He heard her, then. It hadn't taken very long for him to be attuned to the sound of her voice, even upstairs in her bedroom, with its unmade bed, stacks of books scattered everywhere, and the ficus tree in her window growing green and healthy. Last night he had touched the sheets, wondering if she slept with that silk dress against her skin.

"Hello?" She sounded sleepy, and he heard her moving, sitting up in bed, sheets sliding against each other.

He pushed the blanket he'd taken from the closet aside and swung his feet down to the wooden floor. There was silence upstairs. She must be listening to the person on the other side of the phone.

"Oh, no," she said, quietly. "What does the doctor say?"

Another long pause. "All right," she said. "I'll be there as soon as I can. No, really, Yann, it's all right. I'll be right there. Just let me get dressed and get some breakfast. I'll drive out." Then he heard her laugh. It was a sad little sound. "I'll bring a friend. She'll like him. No, I don't think so. I'll be there before noon. Um-hmm, good-bye."

He heard her hang up, and she sighed deeply. Then she leaned over, and he heard the sound of a phone dialing. A pause. He kept his eyes closed, imagining her warm and tangled from sleep, yawning delicately. His body rose at the thought and he clamped his control down. "Suzanne? Yes, I'm fine. No, nothing's happened, except that Yann called me. Tina's in the hospital. He thinks this is the last time. Yes, I'm going. Can you get ahold of Elise and have her open the shop? Yes, I'll take him. He slept here. No, on the couch. Suzanne, no. Oh, for God's sake, I'm an adult. Quit it." She sounded a little more awake. He could imagine her smiling.

What would it be like to wake up to that smile, holding that smile against him?

"No, I'm going to get some coffee, finish some laundry and get dressed. Then I'll go down there." A long pause. "Really?" She sounded serious, now. Dante shut his eyes and imagined watching her bare pale shoulders covered with her amazing dark hair, playing with a strands of it—imagined letting it slip through his fingers. "Knight of Swords." His ears perked, hearing that. "Just like the last one," she said, heavily. "Oh, Suzanne. That's like…"

He heard her get out of bed and pace across the floor. "But it could be something else," she said. "It could be that he isn't…"

It was frustrating, hearing only one side of the conversation. He walked into the kitchen and looked at her coffeemaker. Well, he could make coffee. It was a fairly simple operation.

There was ground cinnamon scattered around the coffeemaker, and he guessed that she added it to the grounds. After a short search, he found the coffee in the freezer. It was gourmet coffee. Of course, he thought, she wouldn't want anything less. He found himself smiling. The dirty dishes would go into the dishwasher. He could do that, too. He was used to cleaning up after himself.

"Well. So he's the Knight of Swords, and he's…You think he's my…?" she said into the phone. "I'm going to take him with me, Suzanne. I trust him."

That warmed him all the way down to his bare toes.

"Well, it's up to me, isn't it? My instincts are good. Even you have to admit that. And if you think he's my Knight…"

Then she laughed. The soft sound made Dante sweat. "Good enough. You don't have to like him, just be polite. If he turns out to be bad news, we'll just get rid of him the way we got rid of Jingle. Okay?" Another laugh, pleasant and low, making his body tighten. He started making the coffee. "All right. Thanks. I appreciate it." Then she hung up and he heard her pacing through her bedroom. "Really," she said. "She's the one that keeps calling him the Knight of Swords. *I* think he's okay, and my tastes aren't *that* bad. He's certainly cute enough."

Dante found himself smiling. She didn't know he could hear her, and she was talking to herself. She probably did that a lot. He had already started to listen for the sound of her breathing, tracking her movements, anticipating her.

He turned the coffeemaker on and was rewarded with the rich, illusory smell of coffee filling the air. He started clearing the counter, and he suddenly stopped, closed his eyes. It was easy to imagine doing this every morning, while she thumped cheerfully through the house, bright scarves of emerald glow trailing her, and the smell of her hair and skin filling the world.

"Well, good morning to you," she said brightly, and brushed past him to reach up in a cabinet and get down two green-glazed coffee mugs. "You are my new favorite person, you know."

He blinked. She was wearing the same green silk nightgown, but her hair was mussed, strands falling forward out of her braid. Her eyes were clear now, unshadowed, and she looked much happier. "Is that so?" he asked, trying not to smile. She looked disheveled—and almost too beautiful to be left alone.

"You made coffee," she said, and smiled at him. "And you know how to do dishes. So you can't be all bad."

"I hope not." Then he cursed himself. He sounded like an idiot. "I'm generally thought of as one of the more easygoing Watchers."

As soon as he said it, he hated himself. It wasn't strictly true. He was known for ignoring anything that didn't have to do with his work—which wasn't exactly an easygoing reputation. He didn't want to talk to any of the other Watchers. He just wanted to survive…and find his own Lightbringer. He didn't want to waste time on idle chitchat.

She was smiling at him, though, and poured him a cup of coffee, deftly transferring her own mug to beneath the basket that held the grounds. "Cream? Sugar?"

"Just black," he said.

"Why am I not surprised?" She seemed to take it for

granted that he would want a cup, so he took it, to please her. "What do you want for breakfast?"

"Anything but tofu," he surprised himself by saying. "No, I don't mean that. Anything's fine. Cereal. Whatever."

"Well, I'll leave you to help yourself," she said, taking her cup of coffee out and replacing the glass pot. She poured a little cream into it, replacing the carton in the fridge and kicking it closed with easy, habitual grace. "I have to get your shirt and jeans dry, and I have to get dressed. Then I have to see a friend of mine. She's in the hospital again..." She trailed off, and the first little bit of worry darkened her eyes.

"I'll come," he said. "I mean, if you'll have me. If not, I'll just follow from a distance. I'd like to go with you. It's my job."

"Who pays you for this?" she asked, her dark-green eyes suddenly uncomfortably sharp.

"Circle Lightfall takes care of my material needs," he said. "Other than that, nothing. They house us and feed us, keep us in weapons. We've got a sort of expense account for things that have to do with taking care of the Lightbringers."

"But don't you ever get anything to spend?" she asked.

He shook his head. "No. Don't want anything, really, except..." He trailed off and took a scalding sip of coffee, burning his tongue. *Ouch.*

"Except what?" she asked.

"All we want, once we finish the training, is to find the witch we're supposed to find," he said. "The one that can stop the pain." He couldn't seem to stop looking at her. "And once we do...Well, it's...We..." He couldn't find any graceful way to tell her that she was stuck with him.

Weak winter sunlight came in through the kitchen windows, highlighting the copper tones in her dark hair and showing the flawlessness of her skin. He saw the earrings she was wearing—the Celtic crosses, again, in antique silver— and the faint blush on her high cheekbones. The depths of her eyes were like sunshine in a forest clearing. The ruby necklace flashed. She was barefoot, one foot tucked behind the other as she leaned against the counter, the silk easy and warm against her skin. His fingers itched and tensed into an almost-fist because they wanted to touch her. Wanted to feel that painful pleasure sliding through his nervous system again.

"So you find a witch, and that stops the pain?" she asked, her forehead wrinkling.

"The way a Watcher...Why we do it, is if we find a Lightbringer who can stop the pain...there aren't any guarantees, but we can...Well..." It was complex, and he couldn't explain it with her green eyes on him and her sleep-ruffled hair framing her beautiful face. He wanted to touch her cheek, to find out if it was as soft as it looked. Wanted to cup her face in his hands and—

"You can what?" She cocked her head, yawned daintily, and pushed loose strands of her hair back.

"There's a bond that happens," he said, aware that his hands were sweating. "It's like..."

"Oh," she said, and comprehension lit her face. "So...Oh." Now she was looking at him in an entirely new way. Not an entirely unwelcome way, either. She was smiling, looking up into his face. "*Really*. Well, as a pickup line, that's the best one I've heard."

"It's not a pickup line," he said, helplessly "It's the truth."

She reached out suddenly, her fingers warm and soft where they touched his unshaven cheek.

He flinched habitually, waiting for the lash of pain. Instead, something warm stole over his skin from her fingers, like a narcotic. It drove him to the edge of his control to stand still while she touched him, instead of grabbing her shoulders and...Gods above, but he wanted to do things to her that hadn't even been invented yet. Her bed upstairs would still be warm—

That was exactly the wrong kind of thought to have. Dante froze, watching her, and Theo stood stock-still. If she made the slightest move, even shifted her weight, he might break and do his level best to *show* her what he meant, instead of just waiting for her to be ready.

She swallowed dryly, staring at him with her luminous green eyes. "Dante," she whispered, and something seemed to hum in the air between them. The deadly thing that lived inside his bones settled, satisfied. "Fire," she whispered, her eyes terribly blank. "I *see* it. They put *fire* in you…and you…"

He grabbed her wrist and peeled her fingers from his cheek. He had to remind himself to be gentle. "Don't look at that," he said. The guilt began, then. Would it hurt her? He'd never heard of a Watcher hurting a Lightbringer, but—

"Theo. Don't look at that. That's mine to carry."

She seemed to surface then, looking at his hand around her wrist, her own fingers hanging limply. Dante was relieved to see her personality flood back into her eyes, so that they were no longer terrible and empty. No, Theo was back behind her eyes. And something else was there.

A flicker of fear.

Dante cursed himself. He was holding her wrist, and without thinking about it, he pulled on her arm. She didn't resist, even when he guided her close to him and slid his other hand around her waist. "It's all right," he said as softly as he could. The coffee mugs vibrated against the counter. "You don't have to be afraid. Not of me."

She was soft and warm, and instead of trying to struggle away from him, she simply sighed and laid her head down on his shoulder. As if she belonged there. As if she had been waiting for the chance to sink against him, lean on him, feel his skin against hers.

Dante's head tipped back, and he drew in a long, shuddering breath. This close to her, the power that shone through her was weaving around him, attracted to the Darkness crouching inside his bones. It was like a drug, only it was like no drug he'd ever had. This was something entirely stronger than any drug he'd ever tasted.

She stayed there in his arms, swaying slightly with him, her body warm against his. He finally dropped his head forward and smelled her hair. Sandalwood and her. His body rose, and he savagely clamped control down. This was too new, too fragile, for him to screw it up now. *Wait. Just wait. Be cool, Watcher. Be calm. Be patient.*

The voice of reason wasn't working. He wanted her.

Finally, after entirely too short a time, she pulled back.

Dante let her, even though he wanted nothing more than to reel her back in against his body, where she belonged. Where he wanted her to *stay*.

"I have to put your clothes in the dryer," she said, breathlessly. "If you're going with me, that is."

"Of course, I am," he said, watching the expressions flitting across her eyes and her expressive mouth. "Wherever you go, I'll go. You think you can stand being stuck with a poor, half-crazed Watcher?"

She shrugged. "I suppose I'll try it," she said, still in that strange, breathless tone. "I'm half crazy myself, they say. I go where I'm led, you know, and I tend to pick up strays..."

"Can I be your stray?" he asked, only half joking. "Kind of like your own junkyard dog."

Theo smiled at him again, and that smile made him wish that he wasn't so patient. Made him wish that he could slide the dress off her shoulders and bend down, find out if her mouth—

*I'm not made out of stone, dammit.*

Theo reached up, her soft fingers on his face, and pulled him down. Her mouth met his.

It started as a gentle kiss, and it seemed to flush his entire body with fire. Her lips were softer than anything in his harsh life had ever been, and before he knew it, he had her between him and the kitchen wall, his hands in her hair, her mouth open and inviting under his. He was kissing her hungrily, greedily. Her tongue moved shyly against his, her hands still cupping his face, She stood on her bare tiptoes, her soft slenderness against him.

Dante broke free, kissed her cheek, the angle of her jaw. She was gasping for breath. "Theo," he said, softly, against her throat. The silk dress was in the way, but he stopped himself with an effort of will, flattening his hands on the wall. They were shaking, he noted with a sort of wonder. *He* was shaking.

"Dante," she said. It was so sweet, to hear her say his name, that he closed his eyes.

"Theodora," he said, tasting her name and the soft skin of her neck at the same time.

"I have to go," she said. "I have…duties. Responsibilities."

"I know," he said. "Me, too. I'll go with you."

She shivered as his lips moved on her skin, and that made him move against her. The pleasure ran through him, a spiked chain of fire turning his nerves into molten steel.

"You have to let me go," she whispered into his hair. He shuddered again. It was too much. He was going to do something he would regret in a few seconds.

He straightened. "Cold shower," he said, a little ruefully. He was almost afraid to meet her eyes, but she pulled his chin up a little, her fingers damp and feverish against his fevered cheeks.

She was smiling a little, a private smile. "Me too," she said, with a little hitch to her voice. "I just met you. This is absolutely wrong. You must think I'm a—"

"I think you're beautiful," he said. "Don't worry. I'm not usually like this either. Just for you. You'd better get dressed, little witch." He was beginning to feel a little bit more like himself now.

She bit her lip. He could see something soft and tender in her face, warring with caution. Of course. She must have learned to be cautious, a girl all on her own in the big bad world.

She backed away from him and then turned quickly, almost running to the door leading to the basement. He let her escape.

For now.

# Twenty-One

Theo parked her green Subaru in the hospital "Visitors Only" lot, and looked over at Dante, who was folded up beside her in the passenger's seat. "Tina will like you," she said, for the fifth time. Nervousness made her voice breathless.

"I hope so," he said, for the fifth time as well. He was watching her and smiling. It was bloody hard to breathe with those black eyes on her and the memory of his mouth on hers. He was just so.... "Relax, Theo. I'm good at fading into the woodwork."

*Oh, I doubt that.* Theo thought grimly. *It should be illegal to look as good as you do.* Then she stopped, amazed at herself. She had *never* thrown herself at a man she didn't know, and in her own kitchen while wearing nothing but a nightgown, too. *I wish I had, though. I could have used some practice for this...*

"But..." She looked over at him. How could he sit there so comfortably? She'd seen the sheer amount of metal he was carrying around. He was armed to the teeth. "The guns," she said, finally. "How are you going to—"

"Most people don't even notice that I'm carrying a glamour," he said. "The ones that can tell know enough to keep their mouths shut. Don't *worry*, Theo. I won't get you into trouble, I promise."

*You ARE trouble.* Theo clamped her mouth shut against that thought. Elise and Mari had done good work. This man was so...

She was going to keep her hands to herself, she promised. "All right." She set the brake and cut the ignition. "I'm not worried about getting into trouble. I'm worried about *you* getting into trouble with the police."

"Theo," he said quietly, looking out the window. "The police couldn't hold me, even if they managed to catch me by some lucky miracle. The normals can't even touch me. Okay?"

She nodded, biting her lip. She scrubbed her hands together, feeling her rings scrape. The wind was up, whistling through the bare tree branches, and there were already jack-o'-lanterns on people's doorsteps. Clouds had moved in, and there was a cold, iron tang to the air. Her weathersense said "snow." It was far too early for snow, but Theo's weathersense was rarely wrong. It would be a hard winter. She glanced nervously around the parking lot, and Dante's hand covered hers on the steering wheel.

"Don't worry," he said, that lopsided smile on his severe, handsome face. His hair was sticking up as if every spike was arranged for maximum effect, and his skin was warm and hard against hers. "It's all under control."

She found herself trying to smile. Her heart was hammering like it intended to leap out of her chest and run away. That glimpse of the thing inside him—whatever the chanting circle of men had put inside him while firelight flickered—had frightened her. She had to close her eyes and repeat to herself that she was in the hands of the Goddess, and that he wouldn't hurt her. That seemed to be the only sure thing, that he wouldn't hurt her.

He'd kissed her as if he wanted to pull her in through his skin. Kissed her like a drowning man.

He was still staring at her when she opened her eyes. "What did they do to you?" Theo asked, the vision shimmering behind her eyes. The fire…and the Dark thing they had forced into him, his voice hoarsely screaming, the feel of stone and blood and iron cuffs—

"They made me able to protect you. I knew what I was getting into," he said, shortly, but didn't take his hand away. "Don't look at that, Theo. That's for me to carry. You don't have to do that."

"Are you even human?" she asked, and was ashamed of herself before it even left her mouth. He'd felt human enough an hour and a half ago. As a matter of fact, Theo had wanted to drag him upstairs and…She shut off *that* line of thought in a hurry.

He only looked thoughtful, his black eyes on her, the almost fully-healed slice on his cheek and the other one under his hairline flushed a faint pink. "I don't know," he said, looking at her, the lopsided smile fading. "Human enough, I guess." And he gave her that hungry look again, the one that made Theo feel a little faint, because she could tell that he was thinking of leaning over and putting his mouth on hers. And if he did that, Theo would put her hands up and touch his face, pull him into her—

The moment passed. He leaned back, and the tension between them snapped almost audibly. "We'd better go visit your patient, little witch," he said, and let go of her hand. He opened up his door, letting in cold air, and got out.

Theo had to sit there for a moment before she realized he was going around the car, probably to open her door for her. She floundered out of her seat belt and was grabbing her black bag when he *did* open her car door. Then he leaned down and offered his hand as if she was Cinderella alighting from her carriage.

*Cinderella was a pagan Goddess,* she reminded herself, taking his hand and getting out of the car. She stuffed her car keys in her coat pocket with her wallet. *The pumpkin is a sign of fertility, and working her foot into the slipper—we all know what* that *represented.* She took a deep breath, slammed the car door, and then looked up at Dante. He was standing there in the directionless, cloudy winter sunlight, hands now in his pockets, watching her.

He'd been watching her all along.

He smelled like musk and leather and iron. His shoulder had been hard with muscle, and a knife-hilt...Well, he had moved so that it didn't jab her. She knew what he smelled like now, and she knew what the stubble of his cheek felt like. She even knew what it felt like to kiss him, melting in through his skin. He had held her quietly, barely breathing, very gently. How a man with so many weapons could be so gentle, so diffident...she didn't know, couldn't guess.

"Why aren't you...well, mean?" she asked him.

His face didn't change. "I can be mean, Theo. Plenty mean."

She grinned at him, suddenly seeing the amusement in his

serious black eyes. "I don't believe that," she said. But…well, she did. She had seen him last night, diving out through the window, a wolf's snarl on his face. He had gone past her, through the window, glass breaking…and he hadn't even paused. Hadn't even broken stride. That spider-thing with the red eyes…

"Those things," she said, turning towards the hospital. He fell into step slightly behind and to her right. "How…how many of them have you…"

"Too many," he said. "The Crusade creates them to hunt, along with the zombie Knights. The Sliders are more common, and there are a lot of other predators."

"Zombie…" She tried not to sound shocked.

"It can be done," he said. "Takes power and some heavy-duty ceremonial magick. They rob graves, honey. The Crusade's been a personal prelature for a long time, and it has hush-hush funding from the Vatican Bank."

"Where does Circle Lightfall get its funding from?" she asked. She glanced at the parking lot and was about to step out to cross the driveway in front of the entrance, when his hand closed around her shoulder.

A pale gold SUV driven by a white-knuckled older man screeched around the corner, turning into the circular drive that led to the Emergency Room entrance. Theo stood, stock-still, and watched the man pile out of the SUV, running around the front. Dante's hand gentled on her shoulder. He was very still, watching.

A very pregnant woman opened the passenger's side door. Theo smiled. The pregnant woman calmly slid down, carrying a small floral duffel bag. "Will you just stop?" she said, loudly enough to be heard where Dante and Theo stood. "Go park the car. I'll go on in."

"But—" the older man said, flapping his hands.

"Go and park the car, Steve," she snapped at him. "Now. Then come inside. Okay?"

"Okay…" He scrambled around to the driver's side again and jumped in. The woman shook her head, breathed in as a contraction hit, and then started walking for the ER entrance.

She made it, and a few moments later, the older man came running pell-mell from the parking lot. He vanished through the sliding glass doors.

Theo put her hands together, bowed slightly. "There goes the Goddess," she said, quietly. "Thank you, Dante."

"No need," he said, and indicated the driveway. "After you, my witch."

She stepped down, and he walked right next to her.

It was comforting, she decided. Like having a guardian angel.

A six-foot tall, very broad-shouldered, black-eyed guardian angel, with enough weaponry to start another world war. A guardian angel who smelled like musk and leather and man. A guardian angel who kissed like a lightning bolt.

*Stop it, Theo. Concentrate.*

She went through the sliding glass doors, forgetting her questions as the feel of the hospital enfolded her. Lysol, human pain, compassion and cruelty, all swirling around her. There were dark spots and bright, and soft little brushes against Theo's consciousness—babies, old people, children, the people in the ER, spiky masses of pain or fear, the people on the surgical floors drowsing with painkillers or painfully frightened.

Theo shivered a little bit, and she could feel the edge of her personal power solidifying. The wards she had built into her aura vibrated and locked down.

"Very good," Dante said. "Nice shielding."

"My wards? Oh, Suzanne taught me," she said, automatically turning to her right. Dante fell into step slightly behind her, following her step for step. "Well, I already knew some of it," she amended. "I had figured out a lot of it in self-defense, so I didn't drown in what other people were feeling. But Suzanne had a method, so to speak, and it helped." She turned aside and pushed open the door for the staircase. "We're going up to the fifth floor."

"Really?" he asked, his voice neutral.

"I can't use an elevator," she admitted. "I'm sorry."

"I know. It's all right," he said. "I need the exercise. Why don't you like elevators?" He followed her up the first flight of stairs.

Theo ran her hand up the chipped blue paint of the handrail. The stairs were covered in green linoleum with little blue flecks in it. "I just...I don't like them," she said. "I never have."

"Fair enough," he said.

"How did you know?"

He made a noncommittal noise. "Most Lightbringers are claustrophobic," he said, and then stopped short, as if he had decided against saying anything else.

Theo wondered at that, but she was so unsettled that it didn't really sink in. "What about you?" she asked. "Do you have any phobias?"

"Just not being alert enough to stop something from hurting you, that's all," he said.

That caused a traitorous little bubble of warmth under Theo's stomach. She looked down at her feet, her bag bumping against her side, and cleared her throat. *A nice thing to say, but I wonder if it's true. Could he kiss me like that if it wasn't true? I know he's telling the truth, but his wards are so good. No, he couldn't lie to me. I know it.*

Theo sighed and kept going up the stairs. Her thighs began to burn, and after the third floor her glutes were beginning to hurt too. *I can always tell when I have a patient at the hospital by the state of my ass,* she thought, her strange morning mood beginning to sour again. She had felt oddly light and free this morning, despite the fact that her sleep last night had been thin and broken by restless dreams of hungry, red-eyed giant spiders chasing her down deserted city streets. And dreams about a black-eyed man, holding her in his arms while he—

The fifth floor door loomed, and Theo banged through it gratefully. One of the nurses looked up from the station and grinned. It was Mary Locarno, a short pudgy woman with a black ponytail and a no-nonsense red face.

"Theo!" she said, and elbowed another nurse. "Sandy, it's Theo!"

Sandy—Alexandra Lewis—was a tall, rawboned older woman. She was wearing a bright-pink set of scrubs and had a little fuzzy panda clinging to her stethoscope.

"Theo," she said, slightly less delighted but still warmly enough. "Good to see you. We've got some little guys in the nursery that could use your magic."

Theo found herself smiling. "Really? I thought I was taken off the volunteer roster when Dr. Georges got all twitchy."

"Naah, Georges is moving to Alaska. Better hunting out there. We were hoping you'd drop by." Mary's hazel eyes moved over Dante, and her smile widened. "Who's your friend?"

"This is Dante," Theo said. "He's escorting me around. Suzanne thinks it's a good idea. She seems to think I'm going to be mobbed by groupies one of these days." Theo heard the not-quite-lie come out of her mouth and was amazed at herself. Dante said nothing, but both Mary and Sandy straightened a little and smiled at him. He must be using that angelic, lopsided grin on them, she thought, and felt something suspiciously like jealousy color her cheeks. *I'm acting like a blushing idiot,* she thought, and firmly took control of herself. "I'm here for Room 506," she said, and watched Mary's face fall a little.

*Oh, no,* she thought. *It must be bad.*

"Yeah," Mary said. "Tina. I'm glad you're here, Theo. Go on, and when you're done, do you think you can stop by and sign up for some nursery hours?" She reached down and picked up a hot-purple clipboard that had a little stuffed koala attached to it. You could always tell the office supplies from the pediatric floor, they were brightly colored and covered with animals or schoolhouse designs.

"I will," Theo promised. "How's Tina doing?"

Mary shrugged. That was the worst thing she could do, and Theo felt her stomach flip again.

"We have high hopes," Sandy said, firmly. "She's a fighter, that girl."

Theo nodded. "I'll sign up on my way out," she said. "Why did Dr. Georges decide to move?"

Mary snorted. "Who knows what goes on in the mind of Georges?" she said, in a sepulchral tone, wiggling her black eyebrows. The picture was comic, and just a little frightening.

Theo found herself giggling.

"Only his golf clubs know for sure," Sandy chimed in.

"Go on, Theo. Good to see you."

"Thanks, ladies." Theo walked past them, her palms starting to sweat a little. *It must be bad.* She continued down the wide, carpeted hall—the carpeting was dark blue, extremely short, tough, and easy to roll IV frames and gurneys over— with the cheerful plates in primary colors stuck to the wall. She knew where 506 was—she'd come and visited little Alison here last year, for a full three months, until Alison had gone into remission—and tapped at the door before opening it inward.

"Good morning, everyone," she said, using her professional greeting, and was rewarded with a soft sigh.

"Theo!" Tina whispered. She was propped up in her bed, and she wore a pink baseball cap turned backwards on her head. Her big hazel eyes were filled with delight. Other than that, the blankets were pulled up over her thin body. An assortment of tubes—oxygen to her nose, an IV in her hand, other assorted wires and gadgets—crowded around the bed.

Theo walked into the room and stood with her hands on her hips. "My, my," she said. "Miss Tina. I didn't know you were a Dodgers fan."

"I'm *not*," Tina said, her pale mouth turning up at the corners. "It's a *Perfect Pretty Polly* baseball cap, Theo."

Her father Yann turned from the window, where pearly morning sunlight filtered by clouds was falling in. He was wearing an expensive blue business suit, and his blonde hair was slicked back. His Rolex glittered, and his shoes were mirror-shined.

"Morning, Theo," he said, wearily, and his eyes flicked over Dante. "Who's the gorilla?"

"This is Dante," Theo replied. "He can wait outside if Tina prefers." She reached into her coat pocket and pulled out a chunk of rose quartz, carved into the shape of a heart. "Dante's my assistant." She slipped the quartz into Tina's small bony hand.

"Does he do magic tricks?" Tina asked. "Like Elise?"

"I don't know," Theo said, and pulled a chair up to the only clear spot on the side of Tina's bed. "Ask him. That's rose quartz. It's good for you."

Tina's eyes were huge in her thin face, and it was obvious that her cap was there to hide a bald head.

She was ten years old.

"How have you been?" Yann asked Theo. "Haven't seen you for a while."

"There was some trouble with a doctor who didn't approve of me," Theo said, and folded her fingers around Tina's thin, pale hand. The little girl was wearing a hospital johnnie and a pearl necklace. "Well, Tina, how are you feeling today?"

"Tired," Tina said, promptly. "Daddy had to bring me in last night. I couldn't breathe."

"Must have been scary," Theo said. She held Tina's hand and felt the healing start inside her. The green light was achingly gentle this time—Tina was tired and sore, and her aura had the sparkling thin luminescence of pain.

"Uh-huh," Tina nodded, but her eyes had strayed to Dante. "Hey mister, can you do magic tricks?"

Dante had examined the room and now stood a little behind Theo, careful not to loom over the little girl on the bed.

"A few," he said. He dug in his pocket and came up with a broad, flat silver coin. "This is a silver dollar. It's bigger than a quarter." He held it between thumb and forefinger, so that Tina could see. "I've had this for years," he continued, his voice calm and considering. "It's a lucky piece."

Tina's eyes were wide. Theo let the power trickle into her, just a little. It would help with the pain, if nothing else. Tina's liver was close to failing, and her lungs were frail. The cancer had returned. Chemo and radiation hadn't helped. It was just too virulent.

Dante held up the coin. There was a single flash, his fingers flicked, and the coin vanished in midair.

"Hey, that's pretty good!" Yann said from the window. "I think I'm going to go get some coffee. Theo, you want some?"

"Sure," Theo replied. It would do Yann good to take a break. Tina's mother hadn't seen her husband or daughter for five years, being too busy in the Bahamas with a string of very rich boyfriends, and Yann had raised his girl and nursed her through two years of almost-constant hospital stays on his own.

Tina was staring open-mouthed at Dante, who smiled and spread his hands.

"Nothing there," Dante said.

"Sweetheart, can I get you something, anything?" Yann bent over his daughter. That brought him close to Theo, and she felt Dante stiffen a little behind her. He said nothing.

"No thanks," Tina said, still staring at Dante. "How'd you *do* that?"

"Magic," Dante said seriously. "Watch." He bent forward, just a little, and plucked the coin from under a thick sheaf of Theo's dark hair. "See? Theo's sweating silver."

Tina laughed. It was the best laugh Theo had ever heard from her. Theo closed her eyes and started to hum Suzanne's song. *Bring me down to the god in the glen, bring me down to the green trees dancing. Bring me down to the Lady's mirror, bring me down to the place of the dance…*

"That's great, mister!" Tina said. "Do it again! Can you teach me how?"

"Maybe." Dante's voice sounded in the darkness behind Theo's eyelids. She felt safe with him behind her. Almost too safe. She ran the risk of being lost in the healing… "If you do everything Theo says. She's the boss."

Tina laughed. Yann kissed her tiny cheek and then left to go get some coffee—and probably throw up in the men's bathroom. He was taking this hard. Theo didn't blame him. His pain was almost as bad as Tina's, and there was no morphine for it. He looked healthy and rich and lucky, and nobody would believe that he couldn't keep a meal down or that he was unable to sleep.

"Oh, Theo," Tina said. "Tell him to teach me."

"Dante," Theo said, "would you teach Tina a magic trick?"

"I'd be happy to," he said, and Theo smiled and let the power come.

# Twenty-Two

Dante drove, since Theo looked paper-pale and had trouble walking. "What do you want for lunch?" he asked her, but she had closed her eyes and was sleeping. No wonder. She had poured more Power into that fragile little girl than Dante had ever seen.

A healing witch. She'd need careful care. It was the second time in a many days that she'd dangerously overextended herself. He had plucked her car keys from her pocket in the hospital hall, as she signed up for two four-hour shifts of rocking premature babies in the neonatal ward. Both nurses had observed her with the kind of silence that visiting celebrities must hear. Tina had looked much better. There had been some color in her pale cheeks, and the pain lines in her young face had visibly eased.

Tina might very well survive, with Theo's help.

Theo sighed. So she was awake after all. "Take a right at the next light. I don't know what I want to eat," she said, softly. "What do you like to eat?"

"Italian?" he asked. "Or there's a sushi place around here."

"You eat sushi?" she asked, opening one eye and looking at him.

"No," he replied promptly, and was rewarded with a laugh. "But I'd do it for you."

"There's a restaurant up the street here, to the left," she said. "Ethiopian food. It will do you good to branch out."

"Sure," he said, and watched for it. There was little traffic on the road, so he could slow down.

*Kemal Ethiopian Restaurant.* The sign was hand-painted and set in a storefront. He started looking around for parking on the street since the small lot attached to the restaurant was full. In short order, he'd found a spot that he could fit the Subaru into with little trouble, and started maneuvering.

"Dante?" She was sitting there with her eyes closed, and he flipped the gearshift to "reverse."

"Hmm?"

"How did you find me?" she asked.

He cut the steering wheel hard left. "The Crusade had you in their files as a high-priority termination," he said, before he thought about it. "We have ways of finding out what they know. They're noisy, and they're so busy trying to stave off the Pope's office and our operatives at the same time that they're getting sloppy. I was sent to stop them and watch over you until it was safe to make contact without scaring you." He inserted the Subaru into the parking space, blew out a breath of relief, and stole a glance at her face. Her eyes were closed, but there was a line between her eyebrows.

"So…" She drew in a long breath. "How did the Crusade find me?"

"I don't know. I'm not a Crusader." He cut the ignition. "What is Ethiopian food like?"

"Don't change the subject," she said mildly, but her shoulders were tense. "So you were sent here. Who else knows about me?"

"It doesn't matter," he said, as gently as he could. "I'm here now, Theo, and I'm going to protect you. That's the only thing that matters."

"What kind of information did they give you?" she asked, dangerously quiet.

He couldn't lie to her. Dante winced and shrugged helplessly. "Just what the Crusade had. Your birth date, your known addresses, things like that."

"And that I'm afraid of elevators?" she asked, and then opened her green eyes and looked at him. The look seemed to slice right through him. "And what else?"

"Some financial information," he said. "Favorite color. Known associates. Nothing about your work at the hospital, or about your—"

She held up a hand. "When were you going to tell me this?" she asked, quietly. "Did you think you could manipulate me?"

"No," he said, immediately. "*No*, Theo. Absolutely not. I had to know what the Crusade knew if I was going to protect you. I destroyed the file. I just—"

"File," she said. "There's a file on me. Someone has a file on me. Why didn't you tell me?" It wasn't just anger he was hearing. It was deep sadness, laced with anger. The car began to tick, cooling off. He scanned the street he'd parked on and the full parking lot of the Ethiopian restaurant. "When *would* you have told me?"

"As soon as I was sure the information wouldn't cause you to do something foolish," he said, and immediately regretted it.

"Foolish?" Now her tone was sharp, the sharpness he'd heard flashes of before. "I must seem foolish to you. Easily led. Easily *manipulated.*"

"No." His voice was sharp too, and it made the car rock a bit on its springs. "I don't want to manipulate you. I just want to keep you alive. You're a *Lightbringer*, Theo, and the most powerful witch I've ever seen. You can tell if I'm lying to you. You'd *know.*"

She was pale, and her eyes were glittering with anger. "How do I know you don't have more tricks up your sleeve?" she snapped. "How long have you been watching me, Dante? *How long?*"

"I told you, I blew into town two nights ago. I was supposed to just watch you and keep you alive until the Circle could make contact. The Crusade's marked you for *immediate termination*. Do you have any idea what that means, Theo? It means *murder.*" He wasn't shouting; he was speaking slowly, and clearly, and in a very soft voice. The windows were beginning to fog. The air inside the car was beginning to heat up. The Dark thing crouching inside his bones was bleeding heat into the air, responding to his emotional state.

"What about you?" she asked. "What do you want to do to me?" She bit her lip almost as soon as the words were out.

He felt the smile spreading over his face, and dropped his gaze from her face to the rest of her. "Nothing you don't want me to do," he repeated. "I just want *you,* Theo. That's all I want."

She let out a long breath between pursed lips. "I don't

know what to do with you," she said quietly, most of the anger gone. The sadness was still there, and Dante felt his heart twist inside his chest. Her eyes were so dark they almost looked brown, and her mouth had turned down at the corners. "I want to believe you so much, but....I shouldn't. You could be anything, and you have *guns*..." Her voice trailed off. "Suzanne says you're the Knight of Swords," she said. "Do you know what that means?"

"It's a tarot card," he said.

"Not just a tarot card," she replied. "He's been showing up in my cards for a year now, moving closer and closer to me. I've known that he was coming...the knight on a white horse, charging into the fray. I don't want a knight, Dante. I don't want someone violent and cruel. I've seen far too much violence and cruelty in my life."

"Well," Dante said, slowly. *It doesn't matter,* he was thinking. *I'm yours, whether you want me or not. I can be as gentle as you need me to be, unless you're in danger.*

"But then," she continued, "you spent all morning doing magic tricks for a very sick little girl. You *were* gentle. So gentle that I couldn't believe you were the same man." Her gaze was thoughtful, and she reached out and touched his hand where it was clenched around the steering wheel. The feel of her skin burned through him again, and he shivered. *Just like a junkie needing a fix,* he thought, shivering again. "There," she said. "There's the Dante I think I know. The other one— the one that had that awful thing done to him." He could smell her. The car was such a close space. Sandalwood and heat. If he leaned over the center console and kissed her now, what would she do? "I don't know, Dante. I just don't know."

"You don't have to," he said. "I'll just hang around, and if you decide that you don't want anything to do with me, I'll disappear. I'll just watch over you from a distance, the way I should have in the first place."

It hurt to see her consider that. It hurt to watch her nod slightly, her amazing hair falling forward over her shoulders. He wanted to wrap his fingers in that hair and pull her across the space between them and *make* her see, *make* her understand.

"If you'll just watch me anyway," she said, "what's the use? No." She sighed, and he felt the rage rise in his spine. *If she tells me she wants nothing to do with me, if she tells me that she wants me to go away*— "No, I think I'll just trust you," she finished. "A year is a long time to wait for this and then dump it. The cards told me that you're an honorable man."

He winced again. He was nowhere near honorable. He'd done some horrible things in the war. He'd been forced into them, sometimes, and other times he'd just *done* them. He wasn't honorable at all. He was an animal, and he'd taken himself to obedience school—and graduated, still alive, with the Darkness inside him and only one chance to redeem himself.

That chance was sitting in the passenger's seat, watching him quizzically. She still looked sad, and he wanted to make her smile, anything rather than this sadness. "The cards also told me that you need healing," she said into the buzzing silence. "And I'm a healer." She was biting her lower lip, worrying it with small white teeth.

"I just want to protect you," he said, lamely. "If you don't...I mean, if you don't want me...I'll..."

"It's all right, Dante," she said, and sighed again. "I want you to stay. I wished for you, and I got you. I'd be silly if I tried to send you away."

"You would," he agreed. Relief made his hands shake a little, and he disguised it by clenching his fingers against the steering wheel. He had to be careful. He could rip the whole column out if he wasn't, and he didn't want to frighten her.

"So," she said, and her face brightened just a little. She took her hand away from his and he almost cried out. "Why don't we go on in? I'll buy you lunch, and you can come with me on my rounds. Okay?"

"Okay," he said. "If you like, Theo, I'd even eat sushi."

He was rewarded with a small smile, and that made the relief crashing around inside him even stronger. She wasn't going to send him away. That was all he cared about right now.

# Twenty-Three

Lunch was a quiet affair. Theo had "soup," which was sour flatbread and hot sauce made with chickpeas and vegetables. She didn't know what Dante ordered, because she was too tired to listen. The food gave her some ballast, and she didn't feel quite so light and wild and sleepy at the same time. She asked for hot tea, and that helped, too.

Dante said almost nothing. He had chosen a table back in a corner and had put his back to the wall. Theo had considered sitting next to him, but then she decided to sit across from him. She wanted to lean against the wall while she ate, since she was a little too exhausted to sit up straight.

She was a regular here, and the cook—a tall, shy, ebony-skinned woman with large sloe eyes—came out and exchanged a few words, looking nervously at Dante. Theo didn't blame her. He looked far too dangerous to be in a normal little ethnic restaurant, sitting down calmly to tea and lunch.

Theo found herself planning out her rounds today. She had just enough time to walk down the Ave and check in with everyone before she had to be at the Cauldron. Elise had opened, and Mari would be in for the afternoon shift. Suzanne would pitch in if needed. Then they would all get together and try to figure out what to do with the two Watchers.

*Correction,* she thought, watching Dante take a sip of water. His eyes had never once left her, not even when he ordered his food. *What Mari's going to do with her blond boy, because I'm afraid I'm stuck with this tall, dark and absolutely scrumptious piece of man.* The thought made her smile, and she lowered her head and took a drink of warm tea. She was feeling much better.

She ducked into the bathroom once she was finished and splashed some cool water on her face. She felt like she'd been blushing almost continually since she'd seen the man. What was wrong with her?

*You've got to hand it to Elise,* she thought, patting her

face dry with a paper towel and straightening to look at herself in the small mirror over the sink. *She can certainly cast one hell of a bring-me-love spell.* The mirror was losing its silver and showed her a pale, disheveled, and blushing Theodora Morgan. She spent a few moments trying to run her fingers back through her long hair and restore it to some semblance of order.

*He likes it messy,* some deep voice whispered to her, and Theo stared into the mirror—green eyes, nose too big, mouth too big, cheeks too high, hair too messy. But when he looked at her, he seemed to see something else. Something that made his eyes go soft and his mouth curl up a little, something that made him…

"Stop it," Theo whispered to herself, watching her lips move in the mirror. Her grandmother's necklace glinted against her throat. She'd worn dark green today, wanting the comfort—a V-neck sweater and a long silk sarong, her usual boots. It was going to be cold out on the Ave. "Pull yourself together, Theo," she said. "You have work to do."

With that out of the way, she used the toilet, flushed, washed her hands, and exited the bathroom to find their table—the one where Dante had sat across from her—was empty. Her coat was there, and her bag, and a twenty-dollar bill, but he was gone.

"Oh," Theo said, her eyes blinking.

She left the twenty there—it would more than cover the meal—and picked up her bag, snugging it across her body. Then she picked up her coat and settled it across her shoulders. The restaurant was deserted, except for the cook and the cook's husband, who performed the dual duty of waiter and cashier. The cook's husband nodded at her as she left, stepping out into the cold.

She looked around the parking lot. No sign of him. Where were all the people driving the cars that filled the lot? Probably across the street at the supermarket that hunched under the iron-gray sky. The supermarket's parking lot was full, too. People probably stocking up for Halloween and a winter storm that seemed to be fast approaching.

Theo reached into her pocket for her keys and discovered they were gone. Of course. Dante had them. She sighed and looked around the parking lot again. Nothing but empty cars.

She stepped down from the restaurant's porch into the parking lot. Dante had parked only half a block away, and she had a spare key in a little magnetic box under the bumper. That had been Suzanne's idea—Suzanne, always wanting to be prepared.

She walked to her car, trying not to think about it. Well, she'd just fallen for a line of horseshit. She would be lucky if her car was still there.

It was. And she was just crouching down to retrieve the key in its magnetic box when she heard something—a scuffle, perhaps. She would have paid no attention to it, except that her nerves were already rubbed raw. She looked up and saw the closed-down appliance shop that stood behind the Ethiopian restaurant, the bank of scraggly holly bushes that were planted between the restaurant parking lot and a small alley that led to the back of the appliance shop, where they used to make deliveries. There was a flash of something in the back of the alley.

The light was taking on the peculiar iron cast of incipient snow. Theo's eyebrows drew together. She heard the sound again—a slight scrabbling sound of effort, a muffled groan or perhaps someone breathing heavily.

Theo didn't stop to think. She stepped up onto the narrow cracked sidewalk and peered down the alley, pulling her coat close to her neck. There was no wind, and the air was still and dead. The alley took a sharp right turn, where the staging area for deliveries was located. That was where the sound was coming from.

The edge of Theo's aura shivered and solidified. Whatever was in that alley…

*I'm tired of being a helpless little girl,* she thought, and walked down the small alley. Grass and thistles crunched underfoot, frozen in the spaces between old wheel-ruts where nothing grew. Theo shivered, moving towards the back of the alley. The building was dilapidated, its windows boarded, and

she heard that faint scuffling sound again. And another sound—
a sound like chiming metal.

She took the last few steps and peered around the corner
of the wooden building.

The pitiless iron light shone down on a scene that she had
to blink a few times to comprehend.

Dante shoved the gray shape against the loading dock, a
piece of concrete that was about chest-high on an ordinary
man. He made a sudden movement, and there was a knife in
his hand. The gray thing—it was about Dante's size and would
have looked like a man, except for the fact that it was made
out of something gray and rubbery, and it had only two narrow
pits for eyes.

Theo's hand flew up to her mouth. The alley was cold,
and the cold seemed to be more than physical. The gray thing
writhed in Dante's grip, and Dante made a low sound of effort.
There was a venomous scarlet haze spreading around him. It
was pure rage made visible, and Dante made a low growling
sound. No, it *was* a growl, and it shook the building he had the
gray thing pinned against.

Dante's knife flickered. The gray thing howled. It was a
loud sound like a train-whistle, drilling straight through Theo's
head. Her knees gave out, and she dropped down, her knees
meeting the hard-frozen dirt and jarring her entire body.

Dante, still growling, tore the knife free of the gray thing
and stabbed again. A viscous green blood bubbled out of the
wound on the thing's chest. It was still making that awful
howling noise.

Dante made a quick motion and tore the gray thing's throat
open. Bubbling green fluid smoked and splattered. The knife
disappeared, and he tore his sword free of its sheath and carved
the thing's head from its shoulders.

Theo gasped. Dante whirled, his sword out, bright silver
in the gray light. He stood there for a moment, breathing in
short, harsh gasps. Then the sword vanished. His black eyes
stared at her, while behind him the gray thing convulsed and
flapped around. It began to stink, a horrible smell that Theo
was sure was more than physical. Her hand was still clamped

over her mouth.

"Theo," Dante said, harshly. "It's a *gimmer*, a Gray. Semi-nocturnal. Feeds on—"

Theo shook her head. She didn't want to know. The thing flopped again, like a fish, and then collapsed against the concrete. Its body was decomposing rapidly, great caves opening in the gray flesh. Theo choked at the smell, her eyes watering. She swayed on her knees, and Dante was suddenly there, holding her upper arms. "Why did you leave the restaurant?" he asked, roughly. "Why? I would have come back for you. I didn't want you to see this."

She shook her head, gagging. Tears trickled down her cheeks. He half-dragged her, stumbling, away from the pile of decomposing stuff that was the gray thing.

As soon as he had her around the corner, the smell fell off a little. He pulled her away from it and out to the sidewalk in front of the building. He glanced down the street, and then he checked her up and down for injuries, holding her by her shoulders. His fingers were hard, but they didn't hurt. "What were you doing?" he asked. "Gods *damn* it, Theo! I left you in a safe place. Stay where I put you next time, will you? You could have...If it had been hunting in a pack...Jesus, Theo, you could have—"

"I think I'm going to be sick," she said, in a high, breathless voice that she immediately hated. She sounded like a whining little girl.

He examined her again and then pulled her forward into a fierce hug. Anyone watching would have thought that they had just had a fight and were making up.

*He killed it. He just killed it. He just stood there and killed something, and he's touching me. He's killed something...*

She retched, but he held her against his chest, a knife hilt poking into her armpit until he moved a little to get it out of the way. He stroked her hair, making a low soothing noise that thrummed in his chest.

"Shh, Theo. You never should have seen that," he said into her hair. "It's all right, sweetheart. It's all right."

Theo shook her head. It was *not* all right. He'd just killed something. She swallowed and pushed at him. "Leave me alone," she said, shoving at him. It was about as effective as shoving at a brick wall. He simply didn't move. He was so warm that faint tracers of steam were beginning to rise from his skin in the frigid air.

"It feeds on kids, Theo. It feeds on hate and anger and the darker emotions. And you'd be a tasty morsel for it, because you're—"

Theo couldn't stand it anymore. "What good is being able to heal if everyone wants to kill me for it?" she screamed. "I didn't want this! *I want to go to Mexico!*"

He kept stroking her hair. "Well, then," he said. "We'll go to Mexico. White sand beaches and nice warm water."

She was shuddering. "Mexico," she whispered. "I wanted to go to Mexico."

"Then we'll go," he said. "Mexico. When?"

"A c-c-couple of months," she said, and then looked up at him. "What?"

"You want to go to Mexico, we'll go." His face was kind now, his black eyes warm.

"You killed it," she said. "You *killed* it."

"I did," he said. "I'd do it again. If that thing had caught you alone, it would have tried to hurt you. It's my *job* to make sure that doesn't happen." The slashes on his face were almost fully healed, shiny with pink scar tissue. He'd gotten those wounds protecting her.

Theo's heart fell into her stomach. She was shivering. "I h-h-have to d-d-do my r-rounds," she said, her teeth chattering.

"First you need to warm up. Where are your rounds?" He was still holding her, but now he looked around the street. It was deserted.

"D-d-down on the A-ave. Univ-v-versity A-Avenue." Her entire body felt cold. Maybe it was shock. *He just killed something. How can he be so kind after he just killed something?*

"All right." He half-carried her to the car and closed her inside it. Then he rounded the car, dropped into the driver's seat and twisted the key. The engine purred into life. They sat there, Theo shivering, waiting for the car to warm up. "What part of Mexico?" he asked, finally.

"Zihuatanejo." she said. "I h-heard ab-bout it in a m-m-movie." She couldn't stop craning her neck to look back towards the alley. The little alley with the decomposing *thing* in it. *Would it be worse,* she wondered, *if it had looked human?*

"Sounds good," he said. "I need a vacation."

Absurdly, Theo began to laugh. He looked calmly at her while she laughed, and then she started to cry. He produced, of all things, a white cotton handkerchief from one of the pockets of his long leather coat. She used it to sob into, and when the car was warm he flipped the heater on full blast. Blessed warmth folded around her, and she sobbed even harder.

"It's all right," he said, finally, when her sobs had dried up to hiccupping little gasps. "That's the reaction I had, too."

"When?" she asked, and wiped at her nose. *I must look like a mess,* she thought, and looked up at him. He was studying the steering wheel, giving her privacy. Or maybe her crying disgusted him.

"The first time I saw someone kill someone else," he said. "I lost my innocence pretty young, Theo. I'm glad you still have yours. You're clean, you know? Clean." He put the car in drive. "Put your seat belt on, okay?"

She obeyed him automatically, clicking the seat belt home. "How long ago?" she asked. "How long ago was your first time?" *As if I was talking about him losing his virginity,* she thought, and choked back a horrified giggle.

"Longer than you've been alive, Theo," he said. "Longer than you've been alive."

"You're not human," she whispered.

"Not anymore," he said. He pulled away from the curb smoothly. "But you are, and you'll grow old, and I'll grow old with you. And when you die, I'll die. That's the way it works." He turned at the next block, starting to work his way down towards the University District and the Ave.

As hard as she tried, Theo could find nothing else to say.

# Twenty-Four

She was quiet until he parked in a pay-for lot next to a gas station, one block up from the Ave. Dante already had the geography of the city pretty well figured, so it only took him one wrong turn to get to the street she had mentioned.

When he cut the ignition, he looked over at her. Her eyes were red, but other than that she was as pale and perfect as a seashell. Her eyes were dark with something he couldn't name, and didn't want to. She was probably reeling with disgust, seeing him kill that thing. It had been a sloppy kill. He'd been sweeping the parking lot, and the Gray had hit him from behind, leaping over the holly bushes. He'd followed, acting on instinct, and the thing had gotten a few good licks in before he had managed to kill it. Grays were tough, and they stank horribly once they were put down, being half insubstantial. The other half was only loosely held together and rotted quickly.

Her long hair was a glossy pelt against her shoulders, and her cheeks were faintly reddened from the cold. She stared out the windshield, presenting him with her sad profile, her mouth turned down a little at the corners.

"Theo," he said, finally. "Are you..." He trailed off. She was obviously not okay.

She half-turned to look at him. "Dante," she said. "You've got to promise me—*swear* to me—that you killed that thing because it would have hurt me."

He nodded. Of course. "I swear," he said. "It would have hurt you terribly, Theo, and probably killed you. It's a miracle you've stayed alive this long. Paradoxically, you're safer with the others, because you're more powerful, but the more powerful you are, the more vulnerable—"

She held up one elegant hand, and he stopped, swallowing his words. *Babbling like an idiot, Dante,* he thought, and watched her eyes. The dark green lit from underneath like a dark emerald held against the sun. "Swear to me," she said, "that you won't hurt anyone or anything unless you're *sure* it's trying to hurt me. Promise me that."

He nodded. "I swear," he said. "I swear on my name, as a Watcher." It was an oath, binding as a Greek swearing on the Lethe or a Puritan swearing on the Bible.

She nodded then, apparently satisfied. Dante looked past

her shoulder at the gas station and scanned the area around the car. It was safe enough. "Okay," she said, and took a deep breath. "Do you think you can be inconspicuous while I do my rounds? You can come with me. Just...don't try to scare anyone."

"I never do," he said. That wasn't precisely true. He'd used his size to put the fear in people before. But for her sake, he would try not to. "I'll try, Theo."

She took another deep breath. "Okay," she said again, and at least she had stopped shivering. "Come with me, then."

"Stay there. Let me," he started, but she was already out of the car and heading for the Ave by the time he caught up with her. "Don't do that, Theo." Her boots were making crisp sounds on the frozen pavement. Dante himself walked silently out of habit, taking care to ghost over the pavement. She had pulled her coat up around her neck and was already shivering. "I can't protect you if you do that," he said.

"Sorry," she said, in a tone that suggested that she wasn't sorry at all. It was the first sign of a real temper he had seen in her, and it made him smile. If she hadn't sent him away by now, she wasn't likely to.

*Don't get cocky,* he cautioned himself. *Who knows what she'll do? She's a Lightbringer.*

"Theo," he said, without thinking, "don't send me away."

As the wind rose from the clouded, infinite sky, she stopped and looked up at him. The rain had dried up, and the cold had come. There would be ice on the roads after dark.

"Of course not," she said, and the relief he felt was almost scalding in its intensity. "I wished for you," she said, and then glanced at the sidewalk and back up at him. The streetlights began to flicker in the premature dimness. The clouds would make night come early. Night—and other things. "So I cast this spell," she said, "and I have to deal with the consequences."

She turned on her heel and started off for the Avenue again, Dante matching her stride for stride.

He wasn't quite sure what to think about what she'd said.

# Twenty-Five

Every afternoon, Theo walked up the Ave. She made two circuits, going from the copper statue of Jimi Hendrix across the street from the small University Park that always had offerings of cigarettes or flowers—and once a whole bottle of Jim Beam that stayed there for a whole week until the cops took it away—up to the blocks of shabby apartment buildings past the Nix Mix Comix store and the Glassblower's Haven across the street from the Creation. Theo rarely missed a day. On summer afternoons she would walk slowly, stopping to look in shop windows, pausing as the Ave rats called her name, walking among them, turning down cigarettes, listening to their jokes and seeing the toll that life on the street extracted from them. Always, there would be the ones that needed her help— a small *push*, a healing, the pain taken from a physical or mental wound—and those that just needed to talk to someone who wouldn't judge or blame.

In winter she walked a little more quickly. There were less homeless on the streets, most of them trying to stay warm in squats and shelters off the cold and wet of the Pavement Paradise, as some street poet had named the Ave. In a few more years, the area would be slated for urban renewal, and the homeless would be squeezed to another part of the city. Theo would probably follow them. That was the way it went.

If Theo had been less gentle or lucky, she might have been mugged or worse during one of the long nights she spent walking up and down the Ave. During the summer she would often spend whole evenings until one or two in the morning walking the Ave and ending up in the Creation before it closed. As it was, none of the desperate touched her. She seemed to have a genius for avoiding trouble. At least, until recently.

This afternoon, there were few people on the cold streets, and the ones that were walking around were strangers and didn't stop to talk. Theo walked down to the Glassblower's Haven and crossed the street, looking in the windows of the Creation.

Sage wasn't on duty yet. The barista was a round man with a black moustache and a stained apron. *Daniel,* Theo remembered. That was his name. She continued down the street, thinking, her chin dropped onto her chest.

It was a good twelve-block walk, and along those twelve blocks for the last four years, she had seen almost every type of human drama. Today, however, with the sky promising snow, there was precious little. None of the regulars were out on the street. She didn't even feel the little tingle that would tell her if someone was inside one of the many stores that lined the Ave, looking for her.

*They must all be inside. It's cold enough. Even the gang members aren't out.*

That was strange, too. None of the gang boys were hanging out in front of the 7-11 or the HipNotez Music Store. The gang boys had territories to protect. It wasn't like them to be off the street. *It must be really cold if they're not out showing their colors,* she thought, and shivered. Even Grody and Taz were gone from their usual cardboard beds tucked in the alley between the HipNotez and the Red Light consignment shop. Terence the Nose was gone from his usual spot in front of the Rainy City Loan, and Guitar Joe wasn't under the Quality Grocery overhang with his guitar case open to catch the coins. There weren't even any shoppers once she started her second circuit. She and Dante were the only people moving on the street.

She finished her second circuit and then walked back to her car, still lost in thought, barely noticing when Dante put a hand on her shoulder to stop her from walking out into the street. When they reached her Subaru, Theo dropped into the passenger's seat, and Dante closed the door behind her. He got in, put on his seat belt, and locked the doors. He already seemed to know her car better than she did. Theo automatically buckled herself in.

"There was nobody there today," she said softly. "Must be too cold. In the four years I've been doing this, it's only the second time that I haven't seen anyone I know on the street."

"Hmm," Dante said. He had allowed her silence during

the entire walk. "Where should I take you, Theo?"

"To the Cauldron," she said. "It's only a couple of blocks. You can park in the lot behind our building." She rubbed her hands together and blew on them.

Dante reached over and took both of her hands in one of his. He only held them for perhaps fifteen seconds, but when he took his hand away, Theo wasn't cold anymore. As a matter of fact, her cheeks were flushed with the heat that had raced through her body, slamming into her solar plexus almost hard enough to hurt and then spreading out to flush her fingers and toes.

She looked over at him, her jaw dropping. "How did you do that?"

"It's fairly simple," he said. "I'll teach you how. One of the few things a Watcher can do *to* a Lightbringer without her permission. Just a simple heat-flush. Helps if a witch has gone into shock." He dropped the car into "drive" and pulled forward—he'd parked in the middle of the lot. Not a very safe position, but at least he was probably sure that nobody was hiding underneath.

Theo sighed and tipped her head back, resting against the seat. *I'll just close my eyes for a moment,* she thought. *I'm so tired…*

# Twenty-Six

It was a short drive. The car hadn't even warmed up when he parked behind the Cauldron. The lot was heavily overgrown. The house on the hill above had let their bamboo grow up and their ivy trail over the stone wall that bordered the parking lot. The Dumpster in the back corner of the lot was held in a pen made of chainlink fencing that had ivy growing through it, and an oak tree grew behind it, bare and leafless but still overshadowing the huge garbage box. The other side of the parking lot was an exit, across from the entrance.

There was a row of dishes by the back door of the Magick Cauldron, tucked well back on a strip of dry pavement protected by the roof's overhang. Obviously for stray cats. The food in them was untouched. Of course, with the Crusade watching the shop, cats and birds would want to avoid the place, even if there were Lightbringers there. Stray cats were exquisitely sensitive.

He parked and then looked over at Theo. Her head rested against the headrest. Her eyes were closed, and her mouth was slightly open.

She was beautiful. The arc of her cheekbones, the lushness of her mouth, her long wild hair...beautiful. Not to mention her legs under the green silk skirt, her boots peeping out from underneath, her fingers glittering with rings and the silver in her ears glistening. Theo's bulky wool coat didn't hide how graceful she was, or how slender.

She had dealt with her first taste of the real price of being a Lightbringer, and she had swallowed anger and resentment, grimly determined to deal with Dante the way she might have dealt with a balky patient.

Dante looked up, scanning the perimeter automatically. Nothing there. The residential street was deserted, the houses sitting quietly, and there weren't any shoppers walking a block down. He looked over at Theo again and lost himself in the way her hair laid against her shoulders, the faint sound of her breathing.

"Theo," he said, quietly, not wanting to wake her, "we're at your shop."

She stirred a little, and Dante did something that he had never done before. He leaned over the middle console and kissed her cheek.

It was amazing to be able to do that, without the iron spike of agony that being near a Lightbringer could cause, to be able to feel her soft skin next to his, the smell of sandalwood and the other indefinable smell that meant *woman*. He retreated back to the driver's seat and swallowed roughly.

He wanted her.

Too bad. He would have to be patient. She wanted nothing to do with him.

Theo yawned, and opened her dark eyes. "Hey," she said, blinking at him. "Did I fall asleep?"

"You did," he said, and an unfamiliar smile was pulling up the corners of his lips. "I don't mind. You're tired. It was only a short way."

She shrugged. "I'd better spend some time in the shop. There's going to be a new shipment of candles, and the book orders have to be sent out."

"Yeah?" he asked, and felt the smile widen. "I can't wait."

She smiled at him and reached for the door handle. He caught her shoulder, stopping her.

"No, Theo. Let me, okay? I'm your cannon fodder. Let me go first."

"I thought you were just being chivalrous," she said, and yawned again.

"Not really," he said, and tried to stop himself from touching her cheek. He couldn't. Soft skin under his callused fingertips. "It's SOP for bodyguard duty."

"My very own bodyguard," She looked at him. "If I don't want to join this Circle Lightfall—" She seemed to be a little less angry now. He hoped.

"Then I'll stay with you," he said. "It's simple, Theo. You're my witch."

"How many others have there been?"

"They weren't mine, Theo." He took a deep breath. "Being around them was painful. You don't have any idea. I just had to keep them alive. They all decided to join the Circle, but if they hadn't, there would have been a rotation of Watchers to find out if another Watcher was theirs. And then the Circle just leaves 'em alone. Most of them end up joining."

"Who runs this Circle?" she asked. Even just awakened, she was smart and practical. He felt his chest tighten.

"A council of Lightbringers," he said. "The Watchers don't get any say. We just go where we're told."

She reached for the door handle again. "That's awful," she said. "You could get killed, and you don't even—"

He placed his hand around her shoulder again. "Let me go first, Theo. You just don't realize one thing."

"What's that?" Her dark-green eyes were sparking with fire. "It's not fair. What *one thing* will make any of this into something that I can agree with? Hm?"

"I was dead," he said, baldly. "Circle Lightfall gave me my life back. I've already *been* dead. That I might die tomorrow taking a bullet or fighting a Seeker for you doesn't matter."

Theo stared at him. Now her wide eyes were brimming with tears. Again. "Dante—"

"Stay put. I'll be right there," he said. He opened up his door, walked around and opened hers. "Come on out, Theo. Let's get you under some cover. I feel a little naked out here."

She looked up from the car's seat, tears tracking down her cheeks. They glittered in the sudden glow from the car's dome light. "Dante…"

He offered his hand. *I'm an idiot. I made her cry.* "It's all right, Theo. Don't cry. Please. It really is all right."

"No, it's not," she said, and took his hand. It was a luxury to be able to touch her, feel the power that shone through her stroke at the thing crouching inside his bones. "It's *not* okay, and I won't have any part of it. If you're…if what they did to you—"

"They *saved* me, Theo. And they led me to you. It's all right."

She pushed her hands down into her coat pockets and

regarded him. The street lamp light glinted in the rich brown of her hair. He closed the car door and turned, wanting to slide his arm over her shoulders but restraining himself. He saw her shiver. The temperature was dropping, even though the clouds were starting to come in nice and thick. Maybe there would even be snow. "Let's get you inside, Theo. It's cold."

"It's not right," she said. "I won't have it. It's not right. None of it's right."

"Theo," he said. "They saved me. I was a wreck of a human being. I was an animal, and they made me a man again. Well, more than a man, but you…" He trailed off. "You make me feel…" He trailed off again, shrugged. "Come on. Inside, Theo. Please."

She stared at him, the tears welling up in her eyes. "But you're walking around with all those weapons, and you…you're so serious all the time. I can tell that it hurts you. And you have to do awful things, and they don't even give you any spending money."

"I don't need anything else," he said. How on earth would she understand? She'd never crouched in a war zone, hearing the shrieks of the dying. She'd never come back from the jungle with a head full of nothing but screams and bullets. She'd never seen the way a Lightbringer shone in the middle of hell. Because it *had* been hell. And the only thing that had saved him was that light, coming through a Lightbringer. "Theo," he said. "You're cold. Let's go in. I'm okay. I promise you."

"I can't believe I'm crying," she said, sounding distracted, and then looked up at him. Two perfect crystal tears slid down her face. "Was it really awful for you?" she asked.

Dante opened his mouth to reply. Shut it. Nodded. "It was," he said, finally. "But it's worth it now. There are things worth fighting for. I've always believed that. Better than rotting at home in front of a television."

Theo's mouth quivered, and he cursed himself. "Theo," he tried, desperately, "most people never find anything to fight for. I'm *lucky*. I was trained to be a killer. This way, at least, I can do something *good*. Don't you get it?"

She didn't look like she did, but she nodded anyway. "All

right," she said, softly. "But I still don't think it's right that
they ask you to do these things and they don't even—"

He shook his head. "Don't, Theo. They gave me more than
I deserved. Now, can we please go inside? You're shivering."

She complied, but on the way down the hill towards the
shop, she slipped her arm through his. "Thank you for being
kind to Tina. And thank you for saving my life. Again," she
said, softly. "I don't think you're a bad man at all."

That made his entire body glow. "I thought Tina would
like little magic tricks. Most kids do."

"She's going to keep trying to figure out that first one,"
Theo said. "I felt the Power, but I didn't see what you did."

"I'll show you sometime," he said, and used their linked
arms to steer her a little closer to him. "If you like."

"Oh, yes," she said. The tears were drying on her face.
He'd made her cry, stupid useless idiot that he was. Circle
Lightfall had been kind to him, kinder than he had ever
deserved. A farm boy going into the Marines, surviving only
through a miracle, and then finding the only place on Earth
where he could use his talents for anything resembling a good
cause. The only thing he knew how to do was fight.

"It's not Circle Lightfall," he finally said, as they reached
the corner of Bell Street and Fourth Avenue. The pristine glass
of the window made Theo shiver. They'd cleaned up the psychic
mess that the Seeker had left, but there was enough of an echo
in the air to make her uncomfortable. Dante drew her a little
closer. "It's you, Theo. I didn't know what I was doing anything
for. I know now. I was doing it for you."

"You don't even know me," she said, stopping by the
swinging glass door. "You just *met* me!"

"I know you," he said, looking down at her. He couldn't
say anything more. *If I was blind again I'd know you. I would
know you anywhere.*

She sighed and reached for the door handle. Dante's hand
got there first. He opened the door for her and shepherded her
in.

Elise looked up from behind the counter. "Hey, sweetie,"
she greeted Theo with a chirp, and gave Dante a cold glare.

"How's Tina? And how are you?"

"Doing a little better," Theo said. "You want to call for sandwiches? My treat."

"You can afford it," Elise said. "We had a run this morning. Seemed like everyone wanted candles, books and ritual robes. We're out of crystal globes. And that incense—the Halloween Delight—we're out of that." She couldn't repress a grin. "Looks like the abundance work paid off."

"It's supposed to," Theo said. Her own smile had come back. The pride she felt in her shop was evident. "Thanks for coming in, Elise."

"Hey, it's my profit-sharing too," the redhead replied. Today she wore a clinging burgundy sweater and a pair of skintight jeans. "Mari called. She's going to come by when she's finished at the library. Ka-*ching!*"

Theo started to giggle. She was struggling out of her coat, and Dante helped her without thinking, hanging the woolen coat up on the big iron coat-rack. The wards on the front of the store were shimmering a bit. He looked out the front windows, uneasy. "She didn't," Theo said.

"No, but she said she was tempted. He is awfully cute," Elise sounded grudgingly approving. "Suzanne's doing some research. She'll be in later, too. Hey, the band's going to be playing at Galaxie next Tuesday. You want to come?"

"Do I have to be a roadie?" Theo asked, hopping up behind the counter. Dante watched the street.

"Nah, you can just sit and look pretty. Hey, what's up with tall, dark and grim over there? He waiting for a bus?" Elise's voice had a faint curious edge.

"I don't know. Dante?" Theo asked.

A corner of his mind noticed and paid attention to her. "Just scanning, Theo. Something doesn't feel right." That corner of his mind would track her no matter where she was in a room. He moved automatically to the side of the door. She was standing in front of the display window, clearly visible from the street.

*They would be stupid to attack during the day,* he thought, *but the clouds are so heavy that the light's failing fast. It's only sixteen hundred. Even this far into fall it shouldn't be this dark.*

The sound of a phone ringing shook him out of his half-trance. Theo hooked up the receiver, glancing at him. The faint worried line was back between her eyebrows. "Magick Cauldron, Theo speaking, how may I help you?"

The sound that came from the phone was a long howl, and Dante grabbed the receiver away from her. "*Suffer not a witch to live!*" a harsh male voice screamed. "*Suffer not a witch to live!*"

Theo took the receiver back with a sigh. She laid the phone down. Elise's hand had jumped up to cover her mouth. "Crazies," Theo said, and shook her head. "Want to call for sandwiches, Elise, or should I?"

"I'll do it," Elise said, putting her hand down. "Bobby owes me a cuppa coffee anyway."

Theo nodded.

"What was that?" Dante asked. "How often does that happen?"

"Oh, pretty often around Halloween," she replied, and Elise picked up the receiver and started to dial. "They're pretty bad this year. But last year we had a woman screaming Bible verse. Just lonely people making nasty crank calls, that's all." She shrugged.

Elise hung up the phone. "It's busy. I'll call later."

Theo nodded absently and then she looked up at Dante. "All right, you big tough guy. Let's see if you can move some boxes."

"Anything you like," he told her, and meant it. He watched her push her dark hair back over her shoulder, and wanted to do it for her, wanted to run his fingers through the raw silk of her hair, maybe touch her cheek and... "Sure. Anything you like."

They spent the next two hours moving stock up into the store, and Theo unpacked boxes and arranged merchandise. Customers flooded in. Dante watched whenever Theo went near the front door, but he didn't say anything, just carried up boxes, alphabetized bookshelves, and dusted things that were too tall for Theo to reach without a ladder. Even Elise unbent enough to kid him about his height and asked him to do a couple of little things for her.

Mari arrived at six, when the shop was closing down. Theo was helping a round woman in a purple coat select the perfect pack of tarot cards and a pair of silver earrings shaped like acorns.

Hanson was right behind Mari. He nodded at Dante over the women's heads. "Honor, old son," he said, coming back to where Dante stood by the racks of candles, his hands stuffed in his pockets. "Guess we're in the same boat. I spent today doing research about the vagus nerve. Did you call in?"

Dante shook his head. "Duty, Hanson. Been a little busy."

"Me, too," Hanson shrugged. "But I managed to call in. And they're sending a pair. I had to tell 'em, Dante."

"I know," Dante replied. "I expected it. Who are they sending?"

"Anna and that hatchet-faced guy that trained Calhoun. You remember, big, tall, dark guy, silent as the grave? Stone, I think."

"I remember." Dante checked on Theo. She was laughing with the round woman, her eyes lit from within and her hair tossed back over her shoulders. Something about a particular tarot deck. "He's a mean SOB. Good backup. Everything by the book."

"Yeah. I'm a little nervous. They threw a whole lot at us last night, and we're not ready for a major offensive tonight, Dante. These three—and the Teacher—it's like trying to herd cats. No regard for their own safety." For the first time since Dante had known him, Hanson seemed nervous.

"I know. I took out a Gray today. Thank the gods it was a solitary," Dante said. "We'll do what we can. Okay?"

"Okay." Hanson's eyebrows lifted. "A solitary Gray, huh? Out during daylight? Well, it's been dark today. *Too* dark." Hanson looked over at Mari, who was at the register ringing up a teenage boy with a handful of magazines and four black candles. "Goddamn, man. Both of us finding a witch here. It boggles the mind."

"It does indeed," Dante said. "You're right. I think something big is up tonight. That redhead's going to be a problem."

"She'll do what Theo asks. You just keep tabs on your little witch, Dante. She's the hub of all this. I have never seen this kind of power before, and I've seen a lot. I don't want to lose any of them. The Crusade's after the green one, but they'll take anything they can get."

"Where's the Teacher?" Dante asked. "She's got some sense."

"I don't know. This worries me. The air feels like a thunderstorm's on its way. The back of my neck is itching bigtime." Hanson scanned the store again, his icy blue eyes dark with thought.

"I know," Dante admitted. The other Watcher hunched his shoulders, running a hand back through his short, pale hair. His blue eyes looked haunted. "We'll just keep them safe until Anna shows up with her hatchet, right?'

"Right." Hanson turned, and found that Mari was looking at him, as Elise whispered in her ear. They broke up, laughing softly, and Hanson's face changed from sullen watchfulness to a sort of bewildered tenderness. Dante elbowed him.

"Keep your mind on your work, Watcher."

"Oh, yeah, like you haven't been playing house all day," Hanson said. "What do you think they're going to do?"

"Maybe a Master," Dante answered. "They're going to start getting desperate. We got two Masters last month, and we've neatly nabbed the biggest Lightbringers I've ever seen right out from under them. They're going to throw a lot at us, as soon as they can. I wonder…"

The bell on the door jingled sweetly. The round purple woman left with a paper bag and a wide smile, and a witch came in the front door, followed by a tall, dark Watcher that Dante knew by sight. He was whip-thin and carried two swords instead of one. His face was straight and severe, and might have been a mask that he had put on and forgotten to take off until it eventually became his face.

The witch was small and delicate. She wore her long black

hair in two braids, one on either side of her face. She was dressed in a long evening-blue gown made out of something silky, and a long black coat. Her power was a weak candle flame compared to the force of Theo's gift, or even Mari's, but it was considerable nonetheless.

Theo turned from the rack of tarot decks, and her greeting was a smile and a cheerful, "Welcome to the Cauldron!" Then she seemed to see under the hatchet-faced Watcher's glamour, and she immediately glanced over at Dante, her face paling and her eyebrows lifting in a silent question.

The warmth that caused under his breastbone was completely unexpected. "It's okay, Theo," he said, and started for the front of the shop. "This is—"

"I'm Anna," the witch said. "Anna Sorenson. I'm a member..." Her eyes traveled all over the store, noting Hanson and the other two witches standing by the cash register. "...of Circle Lightfall," she finished. "This is my Watcher, Stone."

"Nice to meet you," Theo said politely. Mari and Elise, their faces identically shut and waiting, watched from the cash register. "Dante?"

This vote of confidence made heat rush along Dante's spine. "They're okay, Theo. They're here to help watch over you three and your Teacher until we can make some more permanent arrangements, if that's okay with you. Hanson and I are a little worried that the Crusade is getting desperate and will throw something even worse than last night at us. Not to mention the other loose-change bits of Darkness that will feel the confrontation and come by to see what they can snatch up." Dante was crossing the shop almost without realizing it. He arrived at Theo's side and touched her shoulder awkwardly, meaning to comfort her.

Anna drew in a sharp breath. "What wonderful news," she said softly, looking at Dante's hand on Theo's shoulder. "Dante's one of the best Watchers we have. He's never lost a witch."

Theo reached up and patted Dante's hand. Her dark eyes were cool. "So he tells me," she said, and looked up at Dante. "Why don't you invite your friends in, and we'll have some tea. Mari, can you lock up the front and turn the sign? Elise, would you mind making tea? I have questions I'd like to ask, Miss…Anna." Theo's voice was firm. She took control so effortlessly that Dante was a little taken aback. Anna looked a little taken aback as well.

"Of course," the Lightfall witch said graciously. "I thank you for your hospitality, sister." She finally came into the main body of the shop, looking around with bright, interested eyes. "I've never been in here before. I don't know how I could have missed it."

Elise hopped down from behind the cash register. "Well," she said sunnily, "we laid a little spell on the front to just bring in the people who need our help. It's worked wonderfully. What kind of tea do you like?" She was suddenly all smiles, and Dante's eyebrows went up. He knew enough to mistrust this sudden charity on her part.

Stone maneuvered adroitly around Anna, who was suddenly swept up by the redheaded witch. "Honor, Dante," he said, and nodded at the blond Watcher. "Hanson."

"Duty," they both replied, automatically. Then Dante saw Stone's eyes flick over Theo, and he had to suppress the growl that wanted to sound deep in his chest.

"Nice to see you." Dante said.

"You're the most powerful witch Circle Lightfall has seen," Stone said to Theo, with no preamble. "Can you trust Dante? Will he keep you alive?"

Theo glanced up at Dante, who had turned slightly, as if to keep his body between her and the other two men. "I trust him," she said, in that same firm, clear voice. "I'm not sure about you, but I trust him."

"Good answer." Stone nodded, and his face didn't change in the slightest. He might have been talking about a grocery list. "I would trust Dante, lady witch, and nobody else at this point. Don't even trust me. Dante, the Crusade has moved in another two masters and a Bishop. They're out for blood."

"Great," Hanson groaned. "A Bishop."

"What's a bishop?" Theo asked. "I mean, I know what a bishop is, but when you guys say *bishop*, what do you mean?"

"Um, Theo?" Mari asked. She was standing by the front door, one hand on the lock.

Dante was rapidly reshuffling all his priorities. "Do we know *who*?" he asked. "Last I heard the White was in Greece and the Red was in Florida. The Black was in Canada..."

"Probably the White," Stone replied. "Maybe all three. The Crusade knows the magnitude of this Lightbringer, and they want her dead."

"Uh, Theo—" Mari said.

"Excuse me. What's a bishop?" Theo asked again, her hands on her hips.

Mari wrenched the door open, and Hanson shoved Stone aside, almost running. It wasn't an attack, though. It was the Teacher, who came piling into the store with the right sleeve of her camel coat torn off and her silvery hair wildly disarranged. She was bleeding from the mouth, and Theo gasped. Dante slipped his arm over Theo's shoulders and pulled her into the shelter of his body.

Hanson yanked Mari back from the door, shoved it closed, and locked it. Then he spoke a word that reverberated in the air of the shop, and raised a flare of Power that set off a dormant set of shields he had apparently spent some time laying over the entire building.

Not a moment too soon. Dante had Theo by her arm and was prepared to shove her down and cover her body with his own if the windows blew.

Suzanne was gasping. Mari threw her arms around her and was crying.

The impact against Hanson's shields physically knocked Hanson back a few feet. He regained his balance, dropped his chin, and glared at the front of the shop.

"What's going on?" Theo yelled. "Suzanne! *Suzanne!*"

"Get her under cover," Stone snarled at Dante, his face turning into a mask of rage. "Hanson! Get your witch down!"

Hanson triggered the locks on the shields. They would hold now without his control. The air stilled inside the shop, taking on that peculiar dead quality of completely motionless air inside a bell jar. Under Watcher shields, nothing moved.

"Four Seekers," he said. "God *damn*. Chasing her down the street." He made it to Mari, who was checking Suzanne for injuries. "Mari! Are you hurt?"

"N-n-no," Mari stammered. "But Suzanne—"

Theo was struggling to be free of Dante's arm. He clamped his fingers down. "No, Theo. *No*. Stay with me."

"Suzanne!" Theo gasped. "I have to—"

"Get going!" Suzanne gasped, and there was fire in her hazel eyes. "They found me and chased me here—wrecked my van. Four of those things and a man. Tall man with a white shirt."

There was another impact. The shields wouldn't hold up for long under this. They were wonderfully and carefully laid shields, but several Seekers were hitting them with the force of sledgehammers. Someone was indeed desperate.

Elise appeared, throwing her arms around Suzanne. Theo tore her arm free from Dante and ran to the other witches. She dropped down to her knees and hugged Suzanne too. "Oh, no," Theo was saying. "No, no, no."

"Anna, get them downstairs," Stone said, and his witch nodded, a grim expression settling over her pretty face. "There's a temple here, isn't there? I can feel it underneath the floor. If we can get them down and bolster the protections—"

The first layer of shields cracked. Hanson swore. The glass windows of the shop began to spiderweb, including the one that had broken last night. "No time," Dante said. "Take them out the back. I'll buy us some time. Hanson, take Theo and Mari. Cut east and get them under cover. Stone, take your witch and the other two, make a trail and then dive for cover. Got it?"

"Anna!" Stone said. "Get the Teacher and the redhead. Help me."

She nodded, and they descended on the knot of women on the floor. Hanson grabbed Mari's arm and pulled her up. The Seekers crashed into the shielding again. The entire building shook. Dust drifted down from the ceiling, and the floor rocked.

Dante reached Theo and pulled her to her feet. She had her black canvas bag clutched in one hand, and her eyes were wide and wild. "Go with Hanson," he said. He could feel the growl starting, low in his chest. "I'll give you enough time to get to cover. I *will* find you. Stay safe and listen to him; he knows what's best."

She shook her head, but he pushed her into Hanson's hands. He didn't know what Hanson had said to Mari, but she helped to pull Theo away.

"No!" Theo screamed. "Suzanne! *Dante!*"

Hearing her call his name was the worst. Every cell in his body wanted to obey her, follow her, ease some of the fear in her voice. But he couldn't afford to. No *time*. He had to buy her enough time to get to safety.

He turned back to the windows. There was another huge impact. The glass spiderwebbed, slivers fell, and dust pattered down from the ceiling again. Dante flexed his will, and the front door unlocked. It stayed shut—the shields on the shop were independent of the door—but he could see that another two pushes would crack the shielding. Then Theo would have backlash from the shields breaking to deal with.

He drew his sword. The sound of it clearing the sheath almost covered Theo's voice, calling his name again as Mari and Hanson ushered her away towards the back door.

He kicked the front door open and dove out into the street, sending up a flare that the Seekers would see and fasten onto. He cursed as he realized there weren't four of them. There were ten. And that many Seekers meant that there had to be more than one Master.

"*Theo!*" he yelled, and leapt into the fray.

# Twenty-Seven

Theo lay on the brown velvet couch, hugging a pillow to her midsection. Mari sat on the floor next to her and stroked her hair. Mari's blue eyes were wide and worried. She still wore her sweater, and a blue chenille scarf was wrapped around her neck.

Hanson passed Mari and touched her shoulder. "He'll be all right," he said, quietly. "Really. He's one of the best."

Theo looked up at him, her eyes red-rimmed. "What happened?" she asked. "Who would hurt Suzanne? And Dante...and those people? Circle Lightfall? Not anything I ever want to get involved in. I *hate* this."

"It will be all right," Hanson said. "It really will. He'll be okay."

"Oh, shut up," Mari snapped, looking up at him. "Get some tea started, will you?"

It was Mari's house. *Not the best choice*, Hanson said, *but pretty much anywhere in the city's safer now than the Cauldron. I'm sorry, Theo, Circle Lightfall will make good on it.* Theo had started to cry. For some reason, that seemed to make Hanson nervous. He seemed to be trying to comfort Theo, but she could have told him that it was a lost cause.

He went into the kitchen, and Theo shut her eyes. Tears trickled out between her lids. "Suzanne," she said.

"She was okay, Theo," Mari said again. "Really, she was. Just a little bit of blood from biting her lip, and she was tired. She'd run so much. But other than that, she was okay. Just pissed because she lost her scarf."

Theo nodded. A traitorous laugh at the thought of Suzanne without her scarf escaped her. Her hair tangled on the velvet. The house was mostly furnished with castoffs, except for Mari's bedroom. The brown velvet couch had been Theo's once.

"Dante," Theo whispered.

"Well, he was carrying all that hardware," Mari said, practically. "Be a shame if he didn't know how to use it."

"Don't, Mari," she said. "He's not like you think. He played with Tina this morning. Did magic tricks for her for a long time. He was so *gentle*. And I saw the…the things they…did to him…" But the memory that rose for Theo was the sight of Dante with his knife, and the gray thing writhing and rotting and collapsing. She had been disgusted and frightened of him, and stunned by the apparent unreality of the thing she'd seen. She hadn't had a chance to tell Suzanne about that.

"I saw," Mari replied, grimly. "I saw what they did to Hanson. I touched him last night, and I saw something so ugly I started to scream. I saw something so bad that I passed out. When I woke up, he had me in his arms, and he was humming something to me. Something like Suzanne's song, but different." She shook her head. "I like him, but I don't want to be involved with *any* of this, Theo."

"I don't either," Theo said. "But Dante…He…"

"Good," Mari said. She sounded a little happier. "At least he'll keep you out of trouble. And if you're going to insist on treating those junkies and…Well, remember when that scumbag pulled a gun on you? See? It'll be good for you to have him around. He's pretty big."

"He could die," Theo whispered, pulling her knees up a little. Mari kept stroking her hair. "I'm afraid he will die."

"It's all right, Theo," she said. "The Lady wouldn't bring you two together just to kill him now."

"I don't know," Theo said. "She's letting Tina die. And Billy. And there's so much death."

"Oh, stop it, Theo." Mari kissed her cheek. "If you lose faith now, what will happen to us? We need you, Elise and Suzanne and me. Come on."

Theo said nothing.

"Come on," Mari said. "Perfect love and perfect trust, Theo. Trust me. I *need* you. Suzanne needs you. Even the fireball needs you."

Theo took a deep breath and opened her eyes. "All right," she said. The tears were gone, but she knew her eyes were red-rimmed and her nose was full of crying. She felt her usual calm come back. It was a thin veneer over the screaming dark

panic she was feeling, but it would work. It would have to.
"What should we do, then?"

"We're witches," Mari said. "We cast a spell. Get these
jerks—these *crusaders*—out of our hair."

Theo pushed herself upright. "No fury like a pissed-off
witch, right?" she said.

"Absolutely," Mari said. "Elise's cell phone. I'm sure she
was carrying it."

"What about *him*?" Theo asked.

"He's no problem. I've got my scooter," Mari said. "Keys
in my pocket. And my cell phone. We're in business. They'll
meet us, probably at Tantan's." Mari's eyes were grim and
clear. She didn't look like her usual shy, sweet self.

Theo rubbed her hands together. "All right," she said.
"When?"

"Right now," Mari said, and Theo swung up off the couch.
She pushed her hair back and stood up straight, wiping her
cheeks. Her legs were a little bit unsteady, but she could run if
she had to.

"All right," she said. "If I know you, you have an idea."

Mari nodded. "Come on," she said.

# Twenty-Eight

Dante lay for a little while in the gray never-land between consciousness and wounded sleep. It had been a brutal fight. Ten Seekers, four Masters—and a Bishop.

*And a partridge in a pear tree,* he thought, in a sort of lunatic singsong. He'd taken a bad hit. A *really* bad hit. Right in the ribs. The Bishop had brought the shop down around both of them. That would be a duel to remember, if Dante lived to remember it.

Smoke. Smell of smoke and cold concrete under his hands and cheek.

*Theo*…he thought. The smell of her hair. The way she would stop moving from one place to another and cock her head, as if listening. The way she had walked down the Avenue, waiting for anyone in need. The junkies, the homeless. If she could forgive them, could she forgive him? He had just killed five men and ten Seekers. And burned down her shop.

*She needs me,* he thought, and managed to come back to himself.

It *hurt.* The Darkness melded to his bones fed on the pain, but it wasn't a comfortable process. He gasped, levering himself to his feet. Flames crackled and smoke billowed, wreathing around him. He stood on the concrete in front of the shattered, smoking pile of brick and timber and glass that had been Theo's shop.

The tearing agony in his ribs almost made him wish he'd stayed down. He made it to a vertical position and swayed. He put one hand on the brick wall and tried to take a deep breath.

Then he bent over, retching. Clear liquid tinged with red jetted out of his nose, stinging terribly. The pain faded. He must have poked a rib. Hard. Maybe it was the sword-thrust to the side he'd taken—now *that* had hurt like a sonofabitch.

The Darkness was already at work, patching the break and snapping the rib back into place. Dante let out a short growl of pain.

The shop would never be the same. Broken glass, scorching on the floor where Dante had been driven back into the shop and forced to call on some of the less pleasant energies at his command—and the roof falling in. The Bishop had tried to call on some of the same energies, but Dante had been faster. And luckier. And the hellfire escaping his control hadn't helped the Bishop either. Even now he could hear sirens in the distance.

It was Theo's store, and he had been concerned about it.

Theo.

When he came back from the pain of his ribs and lung healing in forty-five seconds instead of the normal weeks it would otherwise take, he stood upright. Ten seekers. Four Masters. A *Bishop*. He'd killed a Bishop. All four of the Knights had been live ones, a particularly foul twist, canny, resourceful, and just waiting to cut out a Watcher's heart. Usually they just directed the Seekers, but once Dante had disposed of the Seekers it had become personal. Masters were dangerous because they could be unpredictable, unlike the zombie cannon fodder. The zombies were only deadly because they were fast and had no concept of pain.

The sirens were very close. Who had called it in? He'd certainly made enough noise, so it could have been anyone.

Dante made it to the corner of the street, staggering. The massive wound on his right thigh had closed over, and, thankfully, the bleeding had stopped. His spine crackled as the Darkness drew on the pool of power available to it, healing him in a matter of minutes. He would be in agony for a short while, but at the end of it, he would be healed. It was one advantage that the Watchers had.

Theo.

Strangely, the thought of her fingers on his face lessened the excruciating pain of healing. He suffered, but only because he had been defending her. And that was worth suffering for.

He had Theo's car keys in his pocket. He'd never given them back. She hadn't asked.

Her shop was gone. Ruined. She would...

Where would Hanson take her?

It didn't matter. He could find her anywhere. Already he

felt the faint flickerings of her whereabouts inside him. Once the Darkness finished healing him, it would tell him where she was. She was his witch, and not even hell itself would hide her from him.

He had ended up six blocks away from the shop, temporarily drawing the Seekers and the Masters after him. Then, when they had realized their mistake, they had doubled back for the store, and he had picked off half of them as they had worked their way back to the shop. Stray predators would be attracted to the scene of the fight—carrion eaters, different things. He would have to be careful with Theo around here, if she wanted to rebuild her shop. The Crusade wasn't the only danger.

The long, nightmarish stumble back to Theo's car took on the same quality as a fever-dream—small flashes of lucidity interspersed with bouts of incredible pain. When he finally reached the green Subaru and dropped into the driver's seat, the smell of Theo still lingering in the car gave him more relief than the fact that the Darkness had finished repairing most of the damage inflicted on him.

He started the car and then closed his eyes, leaning forward with his forehead on the steering wheel. He waited.

The little flickering inside his chest that told him where Theo was wavered and then stayed steady. East, like he had told Hanson. She was on the move, though.

Where could she be going?

Dante slipped the car into "drive." He was going to find out. The Crusade wouldn't keep him from Theo. Nothing would.

# Twenty-Nine

The wind twisted Theo's hair in knots as she hunched behind Mari on the back of the scooter. Mari hadn't explained her plan, but four years of working magick, and working physically close to each other at the same time, had given all four of them a sort of telepathy. Almost like sisters, or identical twins.

Well, the cell phones helped, too.

When they pulled up outside Tantan's, the little pub frequented by college students and intellectual wastrels, they saw Elise standing in the doorway, talking to the bouncer. He was a burly, leather-dipped biker, with a long braid in his beard and little black eyes that sparkled as soon as he saw Theo and Mari dismounting from the scooter, tangled and cold. The air was as frigid as knives, and their breath made clouds in front of them.

Elise waved them over. "Good," she said. "We've got the back room all to ourselves. It would be better if we could do this at the shop, but..."

Mari hugged her. "How's Suzanne?"

"Pissed. She lost her scarf. We ditched the Circle Lightfall people at her house. Idiots." Elise snorted. "Theo, you okay?" Her green eyes were sparkling.

"Kind of," Theo said, and pushed past the bouncer into Tantan's darkness and cigarette smoke. Elise and Mari followed.

The bartender, a skinny man with a pierced upper lip, nodded at Theo through the haze, and someone called her name, but she simply waved and moved on. The "back room" was for regulars who needed privacy, and getting the key from the grubby bartender was a mark of high prestige. Theo simply knocked and walked in.

It was small, a brick-walled sanctum. Elise and Suzanne had already draped the small circular table with a swathe of green material and lit white novenas on the shelves along the walls. The only door leading into the room banged shut behind Theo.

Suzanne straightened from where she was leaning against the wall. "Hello, Theo," she said, quietly. "I didn't have a chance to say that earlier."

Theo smiled at her. "I thought you'd been hurt," she said. "Or killed."

"No," Suzanne said. "Just frightened half out of my mind and with a bloody lip."

"I'm sorry," Theo said immediately. "I should have—"

"It was," Suzanne said dryly, "a valuable experience." She held her arms out.

Theo went into them gratefully and laid her head on Suzanne's shoulder. "Mari thinks we should cast a spell," she said, against Suzanne's shoulder. "But she hasn't said what kind."

"I've done some research," Suzanne said. "It was difficult to find out anything—these people believe in secrecy—but I finally made a few phone calls and called in a few favors."

Elise and Mari came in and shut the door. Elise was carrying a bottle of rum.

Theo took this in. "Oh," she said. "*That* kind of spell."

"No, it's not as bad as it looks," Elise said. She set the bottle down on the table. "Really. I don't mind doing that kind of spell. I kind of like kicking ass, but I think Suzanne's got something different up her sleeve. This is just to bolster me afterwards."

"I've got a map of the city. I don't think we'll need it," Suzanne said. "There are some things you should know."

They gathered around the table, and Suzanne winced a little as she lowered herself down into a folding chair. Elise remained standing and paced back and forth in front of the door, her arms crossed and a smell like burning insulation trailing her. Mari put her hands on the tabletop and the entire table jumped a little, like an obedient dog. The bottle rattled, but it stayed where it was. "I've never gotten used to that," she said, staring down at the table. "Okay. What have you got, Suzy?"

Suzanne's elegant nose wrinkled. She'd rebraided her hair, and it hung in a silver rope down her back. "Circle Lightfall is not what it claims to be. It is far, far more. They do specialize in finding what they call 'Lightbringers,' and they do honestly believe they are going to bring about a new civilization. What they didn't tell us—presumably because we were not ready to know—concerns the Watchers." The air in the room started to swirl, responding to the power of the women.

Mari shuddered. "I saw that they did something awful to Hanson. They put something *in* him, something that burned." The candles shivered.

Suzanne nodded. "The Watchers have taken a page from the Crusade's book," Suzanne said. "And the Crusade *does* exist. It is not as they told us. It's worse. The Crusade has acquired new purpose in this time of the Old Religion reawakening, and their Pope is old and weak and stricken with disease. And it's not just the Crusade. There are predators, stray bits of Darkness in the world, as well as the accidents of Fate, and the Watchers are sent to guard against such things. But they do so with a darkness to equal the Dark that hunts those of the light." Suzanne took a deep breath. "They have things inside them. *Dark* things. The Watchers wait for men that have grown to need killing like a junkie needs a fix. And yet the men they choose are tortured by the acts they have committed and are searching for redemption. So the Dark, that ever yearns for light, redeems itself by watching over the Light."

"This is all very nice," Elise said. "But how are we going to stop these guys from taking over our lives? The shop's probably torn to bits, and the insurance won't—" Her hair snapped with static. The candle flames shivered again.

Theo stretched out her hand. "Elise," she said, softly. "This is important."

Elise stopped, her hair raying out around her head like a halo. "Let's just cast the fucking spell and get going, okay? We've *got* the power, so let's use it to get rid of all this…" She stopped, and clamped her hand over her mouth.

"Right," Theo said. She pointed at the chair next to Mari.

"Now, come sit down."

Elise did, pushing her hair back. "Sorry," she said. "I'm just…I don't know." She was wearing a garnet necklace, dark drops of red against her pale porcelain throat. "Okay. So these Watchers are badasses because they have things living inside them. They're supposed to complicate the lives of women like us."

"We tried living the peaceful way," Mari said. "It didn't work. Maybe we should fight back."

"Better the Darkness is properly controlled than thrashing around and causing great harm," Theo said. She was thinking of Dante. So much power, and so thinly controlled.

"Dark and Light are both halves of the universe," Suzanne said. "And in every human heart. Easy to think we can control it. Can we control a nuclear warhead?"

Elise sighed, rolling her eyes. "Suzanne," she said crisply, enunciating each syllable. "Please, I'm begging you, can you get to the fucking *point*?"

"This city is our home," Suzanne said. "I suggest we invoke the Lady and make this city our territory."

Silence fell on the room.

Suzanne took a deep breath. "It will tie us here—no moving, no vacations. We'll be tied to the city and its protection. We'll be the Guardians of this place. It's a heavy responsibility."

Elise looked at Theo. The question was etched on her face. Mari looked at Theo, too, her blue eyes shadowed in the candlelight and her curls falling forward over her forehead.

*White sand beaches,* Theo thought. *Warm water. And a suntan.*

"Well," Theo said, "I'm tired of moving around all the time anyway. This place is home."

Mari's mouth trembled a little. Elise swallowed visibly.

"Making ourselves Guardians…What good does that do?" Elise asked.

"It means we can ban the Crusade from our city," Suzanne said. "The magick they use won't work in a city protected by Guardians. Most witches don't have the power to become

Guardians. We do. I found an old copy of the spell today, in the library of a friend."

"What's the price?" Mari asked. "There's always a price, isn't there?" She bit at her lower lip, staring at the single white candle in the middle of the green-draped table.

"We won't be able to leave," Theo guessed. "And if they come back…they won't be able to enter. And if they do, they'll have to fight us for control of the city. It means we fight a defensive war. Do they have enough resources to withstand a long siege?"

Elise stared at her, her jaw threatening to drop. Theo glanced over at the red-haired witch, and grimaced, her face feeling frozen.

"What?" she said, sounding aggrieved. "I read military history. I'm not just an airhead, you know."

Elise laughed nervously, her hand over her mouth like a little girl.

Mari sighed. "Come on, you two," she said. "We don't have a lot of time. If those spider things—and their Crusade— could find Suzanne, they can find all four of us together. I don't want to be trapped in here with those things coming after us." She shivered, her blue eyes wide and dark.

"What do we need to do?" Theo asked Suzanne.

"Well, casting a circle would be a good start," Elise said, practically. "Right?"

"That is correct," Suzanne said. "Are we agreed?"

"What else do we have to pay?" Mari said. Her blonde curls fell forward into her face, and she stripped them back impatiently. Theo's fingers came up and found her grandmother's necklace. It was the only thing that had survived her travels. The only thing left to remind her of her parents. The silver was cool and hard and reassuring under her fingertips.

"Not much," Suzanne said. "Not much at all."

"Now wait a minute," Theo said. "Just one minute. Not much? What do you mean, not *much?*" The candle flames shivered again. The back of Theo's neck began to prickle.

"One of us will be chosen to cross over and watch the

border of the city from the other side of the Veil," Suzanne replied.

The silence came down again. All three of them stared at Suzanne, who met Theo's eyes squarely.

*White sand beaches,* Theo thought. *Warm water. Suntan.* "You mean *die?*" Theo shook her head. "Oh, no."

There was a polite knock on the door, and the women all leapt to their feet. Elise's fingers snapped with sparks, and the air was suddenly hot and close. The doorknob jiggled, and Mari took a deep breath.

Dante opened the door.

He looked like hell. His hair was matted with blood, and three-quarters of his face was darkly bruised. His T-shirt was torn, showing pale skin, and his jeans were wet with blood and assorted other fluids. His long coat hung from his shoulders, limp and worn. "Good evening, ladies," he said, calmly. "Sorry to interrupt. Might I suggest moving to a safer place? You're terribly exposed here."

His black eyes fastened on Theo. He looked right through her, as if she didn't even exist. Theo sat there, frozen, her hands lying on the table. "Theo," he said, softly. "This is foolish. Can I take you all somewhere safe?"

Suzanne looked around the table. She didn't even have to raise an eyebrow. Telepathy again.

Theo's hands were shaking. *Dante.* "I'm in," she said tonelessly. "I have to be, don't I? We have no choice."

"I'm in," Mari whispered. "I'm scared to death, but I'm in."

Elise snorted. But the whites of her eyes were showing, like a horse's, and the crackling sparks around her hands didn't fade. "Well, I can't let you guys go into this and be a chicken. I'm in."

Suzanne nodded. She looked far older than she ever had before. "I wouldn't have mentioned it if I wasn't ready."

"Come in, Dante," Theo said. *White sand beaches. Warm water. Daiquiris on the porch...* " And shut the door."

# Thirty

Dante came in, followed by a very pale and rumpled Hanson, who strode across the rough cracked concrete floor and grabbed Mari by her shoulders. "You brainless little...You could have...Why didn't you..."

Elise's fingers snapped again with sparks. She erupted up from her seat and tore Hanson's hands away from Mari. The legs of her chair scraped the floor, and she drew herself up to her full height, her hair a wild aureole around her face. "Don't you *dare—*" she began.

Hanson took one step back, brushing Elise's hands away. "That was incredibly foolish," he said, icily, his pale eyes fixed on Mari again. Elise stood in his way, but it was as if she wasn't even there. Dante's skin began to tingle with the power running through the room. Most of his attention, however, was taken up with Theo.

Dante leaned against the shut door. He saw her tangled hair and her flushed cheeks, and it threatened to stop his heart, she was so beautiful. And alive. He had feared the worst. He *never* wanted to experience anything like the few moments of gut-wrenching panic he'd experienced as soon as Hanson had told him that Theo and Mari had disappeared. "I agree," he said. "Why did you leave Hanson, Theo? I asked you to stay with him."

"We have an idea," Theo said, pushing her hair back. She sat frozen to her chair, looking at him. Or at the blood in his hair and the bruising on his face. He probably looked worse than he ever had in his life.

He was having trouble caring. She was alive, thank the gods. Alive.

"You're hurt..." She trailed off, as if she couldn't find anything else to say.

He shrugged. "It's not bad." She didn't have to know. He wanted to break the news to her gently, but he couldn't. He'd failed her. The shop was in ruins. "Why, Theo? Why?"

She looked down at her hands. Then she looked back up at him. "I was afraid you could die."

"Only of worry when you break cover and go off without anyone to protect you. Don't you understand what is going on? You could *die*, Theo, or get seriously hurt, if you're lucky." He heard the harshness in his voice and stopped, taking a deep breath. He had found her. It was going to be okay. If he had needed any proof that she was his witch, this would have done it. He had found her.

"We're going to cast a spell," Theo said. "We need some time." She didn't even mention the shop. Dante was grateful for that, at least.

Dante looked at Hanson. "Well," he said, relief making his voice clipped and harsh. "If you need time, my witch, time you shall have."

Hanson straightened. "Should I call Anna and her Watcher?" he asked, looking to Dante. Dante was glad of that. Hanson was mad enough to try to hurt anyone who barred his way to Mari. But now he was thinking, and if he was thinking, he wouldn't do anything stupid. Or, at least, Dante hoped.

He opened his mouth to reply, but Theo said, "No. We want time to ourselves. You can stay and watch the door, but Mari and I have decided we don't want anything to do with Circle Lightfall. Not after what they've done to you. So you two can stay, but we don't want them."

Dante took a deep breath, counted to five, took another deep breath, and counted to ten. "Very well," he said through gritted teeth. His side ached and his fingers were crackling with dried blood. He bowed his head. "Just do it, Theo. And then we'll talk."

She pushed her chair away from the table and stood, swaying a little unsteadily. "It's a spell to make us the Guardians of the city," she said, with no apparent expression. As if she considered it no big deal.

Dante felt the blood drain from his face. "You have no idea—" he began.

"That way we can bar the Crusade from our city," Theo said. "We can make this a safe place. Your Lightbringers can come here and not have to fight. We can start that peaceful world you want, right here."

"Making you the Guardians of the city will effectively tie you here," Dante pointed out. "And not only that, but the Crusade isn't the only danger for you. You know about the other Dark things that can hunt Lightbringers, don't you? And the spell requires a willing sacrifice. What about *that*, Theo? Which one of your friends will you sacrifice?" He heard the rage in his voice and took a deep breath. It failed to calm him down.

"None of them," she said, and straightened under his gaze. "I'll go, if necessary. The Goddess will choose one of us, and I'm ready."

"Me, too," the redhead said.

"Me, too," Mari whispered. There were fever spots in her cheeks and her curls were waving wildly, rich gold in the candlelight. The candles were burning with flames at least four inches high, spurred by the Power in the air.

"And I, as well," Suzanne finished briskly.

Dante felt his entire body shiver. "I don't want to lose you," he said to Theo, as if she was the only person in the room. "Please, Theo. I'll follow, wherever you go."

She stood, straight and slim, her long hair tangled and her eyes dark with power. "I don't want to be chased by the Crusade for the rest of my life. And I love this place. It's my home. I've moved around all my life, and I don't want to move anymore. I've finally found a place where I belong. If I can make it safer."

"Theo," he tried again, "You could *die*. If you die, I die."

She shook her head, her lips pursed together.

"We should get started," Elise said. "That is, if none of you guys have a *problem* with us doing what we're going to do."

Hanson folded his arms. He was staring at Mari, who was looking down at her sneakers. "You're really going to risk your life rather than join Circle Lightfall?" His pale hair was mussed, and there were dark circles under his blue eyes. "What if you change your mind five years from now, when you can't move to a different college because you're tied here?"

"Then I'll deal with it," Mari flared, putting her hands on her hips. "And if you don't like it, you can—"

"We're *wasting time*," Elise said, tapping her foot. "Are we going to do this, or not? I mean, I'm having trouble keeping my nerve up here."

"Someplace safer," Dante suggested. "Please, Theo. Please."

Theo turned back to the other three women. "My vote is for now," she said. "We'll never have a better opportunity, not unless we wait and plan. And how many of these spider-things—or zombies, or whatever else is going to start coming after us—are we going to have to deal with in the meantime?"

"You're preaching to the choir," Elise said. "Let's cast the circle and get down to business. If I'm going to die, I want to get it over with." She swallowed visibly. Maybe she wasn't as cool as she wanted Dante to believe.

"I couldn't agree more," Suzanne said. Her face looked old, graven with lines.

"You don't have to stay," Mari said to Hanson.

"The hell I don't," Hanson growled. His icy eyes were alive with blue fire. "Fine. Cast your spell. We'll talk about this later. Dante, let's go set up a perimeter."

"No need," Dante said. The air was pulsing with Darkness. "The Crusade's here. Masters, and maybe another fucking Bishop." He stepped over to Theo, who stood with her head held high, so beautiful it threatened to stop his heart. Even with her hair tangled and her face pale and her dark eyes shadowed with fear, she was the most beautiful thing he had ever seen. "Cast your spell," he said, cupping her face in his hands. Her cheeks were soft in his callused palms, and there were tear-tracks on her face. His heart twisted. She shouldn't have to be afraid. He'd failed her. "I'll buy you whatever time you need. And when it's over, we'll talk. All right?"

She said nothing, but her eyes were full of something he had never seen before. The pleasure of touching her blurred through him, and Dante bent down and pressed his lips to hers.

Her mouth opened, and she kissed him softly, her tongue

moving shyly against his. She was warm, but he was scorching, and he had to force himself to let her go when the screams started behind the door in the brick wall. "Cast your spell," he repeated, whispering, "Theo."

"Dante," she whispered, but he had already turned away. Hanson had his guns out, silver glittering in the gloom. The blond Watcher looked fey and dangerous in the candlelight that did nothing to illuminate the sudden awful darkness that stole into the room.

"Come," Suzanne said. "Take your places."

Dante opened the door and stepped out into the bar. Hanson was right behind him. Dante's sword slipped free of its sheath.

People were screaming and scrambling for the door. Dante didn't blame them. They probably couldn't see the Seekers—except for one pale, gray-eyed girl with a fall of curling black hair. She stared at the Seekers, her mouth opening slightly, with something like bemused wonder painted on her sharp catlike face. She was being ushered towards the door by a tall man with amber eyes and short dark hair, and he wasn't human.

Dante ignored them, scanning the bar. Even the humans who couldn't see the Seekers would feel them. But the Knights, four of them—two live, two zombies—in white vests and long dark coats, and semiautomatic pistols, were enough to make the good citizens run for cover. Not to mention the Red Bishop, a tall, thin, graying man who stalked into the bar wearing long red robes, a miter, and his hands full of hellfire, making Dante's skin prickle with recognition.

Dante showed his teeth. He'd already had one fight tonight and didn't want another one. That didn't matter. What mattered was that Theo was behind that door, and she needed time.

Hanson started firing.

# Thirty-One

"You start us, Theo," Suzanne said calmly. "In perfect love and perfect trust."

"In perfect love, and perfect trust," the three others replied. Mari's voice trembled, and her eyes were fever-bright. Theo had to clear her throat twice.

The power began to coil around them, firefly sparkles against the dark in the air. They stood, four women around a small round table draped with green, their faces bright and sad at the same time. Theo nodded. They were holding hands, and the familiar pressure began under her breastbone. Power rising. The first time she'd felt it with them, it had given her an awful headache. But even then, she couldn't stop smiling. The joy of *belonging* lit in her again, a fierce passionate pride that they loved her and needed her.

"I call upon North, the power of Earth," Theo began. Her voice trembled, halted, firmed. "I call upon Gaia, the great Protectrix. I call on the power of root and branch, leaf and flower. Be here now."

"*Be here now,*" the women chorused.

Theo looked at Suzanne. Suzanne's eyes were closed. She was standing stiffly, and her hand was cold in Theo's. "I call upon East, the power of Air," Suzanne said. "I call upon Athena, great warrior and clever one. I call on the power of flight, of wind, of word. Be here now."

"*Be here now.*"

"I call upon South," Elise began, and her voice was rolling and powerful. Sparks flew from her eyelashes as she blinked, a fierce smile spreading across her face as she said, "the power of Fire. I call upon Sekhmet, the power of battle. I call on the power of will and volcano, passion and lightning. Be here now."

"*Be here now.*"

"I call upon West," Mari said. Her hand was warm but trembling in Theo's. "The power of Water. I call upon Tiamat the Maker of Storms. I call on the power of tsunami and flood, steam and ice. Be here now."

Theo blinked. Mari was usually the gentlest of them all. But it was her choice to invoke a Goddess of destruction. Let it be. *Let it be.*

A blinding flash of silver light cracked in the air in the center of the table. It resolved into a spinning silver vortex, shaped like a tornado, and wind began to pull at Theo's hair. Suzanne's hand gripped hers tightly, but it was cold. The power hummed through Theo's body, burning, and she gave herself up to it. Her heart pounded, and her eyes watered furiously, so she closed them. The sound of the wind in the small room was deafening, and yet she heard Suzanne calmly begin the spell.

"It is our will to take up the power," Suzanne said. Her voice seemed far too loud and clear for this small space. Wind whistled and roared, and Theo tasted lemons, felt wind under wings downy with feathers, saw the light take on a golden cast. "The power to protect our city, our home, from those who would destroy us. It is our will to take up the mantle of Guardians. It is our will to pay the price for this power, in blood. It is our will to do this in love and in trust."

"Perfect love," Mari said. Now her voice was rolling with power too, the power of ocean tides. Theo smelled salt, heard gulls crying, felt the brush of salt wind on her cheek.

"Perfect trust," Theo heard her own voice reply. Her own voice was tree and rock, green living things—and a landslide, an earthquake, black soil that could grow a crop or swallow a city whole. The light turned green, a deep shifting green like the sky seen through a canopy of leaves on a summer day. Her eyes were closed, but suddenly, she *saw.*

Her shop, the Magick Cauldron, its door open, golden light welcoming the desperate. Her home, its white trim freshly painted, sitting in its garden, quiet and sleepy. The Creation, with Sage behind the counter swearing at the balky espresso machine. The Galaxie, where Elise's band played, its cavernous space hung with glittering trails of plastic, the dance floor empty and at the same time, pulsing with people. Suzanne's house set behind its frowning brick wall. Mari's favorite table at the University Library, books piled on it, and Mari's golden head propped on her hand as she studied a sheaf of paper. Elise singing into a microphone, sweat beading her bare skin. Suzanne turning from a shelf of jewelry and smiling, her silvery hair caught in a coronet atop her head and her yellow scarf fluttering. Suzanne riding a bicycle in Maclin Park on a fall day, her yellow coat matching some of the fiery leaves that fluttered in the crisp wind. Mari, kneeling at the edge of the river, her hair lifted by a summer breeze. The river responding to Mari's voice, ripples and swells spreading out, Mari's face lit with joy. Elise, staring into a fire, her eyes dancing with light. Her hair snapping and crackling as she sang, her voice warm and golden like honey.

Theo saw her garden, every plant and worm and insect in it outlined with golden light. A great swell of love burst inside her for this place—the city she had come to four years ago, exhausted from moving yet again—her eyes hot and grainy with unshed tears.

Suzanne's hands tightened on hers. She was chanting something. Theo listened for a moment, joined in. Her voice rose and fell with Suzanne's, offering her love of this place, her willingness to sacrifice herself for its defense. The way the wind moved overhead, clouds massing as the power pulled on the threads of earth and sky.

*White sand beaches,* Theo thought. *Warm water.* She offered that up too, that quiet dream, the sun and the sea and the sky.

There was a shuddering blow against the door, but Theo barely noticed. Her entire attention was on the spell, the way it was taking shape inside the circle of women, the silver light suddenly harsh, so bright that every shadow looked as if it had been cut from black paper. The power didn't come from Theo. No, it only rode her, like a horse, used her as a door, burned her down to ash.

Theo started to scream.

# Thirty-Two

Dante met the blow squarely, threw the Red Bishop back with the force of his own strike. Hanson was yelling, two Seekers and a Master on him. The Bishop Dante was facing was blank-faced, his lips writhing as foam flew from his mouth. His miter had fallen off, but he still had a sword, and apparently knew how to use it, when he wasn't a howling berserker. The Crusade used drugs and fanaticism and pain to make their warriors, picking up junkies and thugs and putting them through the indoctrination with a cocktail of substances that would make the CIA experiments look like child's play. And as bad as the Knights were, the Bishops were worse, because they had *chosen* to be what they were.

There was the clash and slither of metal. The howl of sirens. No, the police would be kept away. The Crusade wanted to keep everything under the radar of the authorities. It would cause an uncomfortable amount of attention, especially since the Crusade didn't "officially" exist except as an antiquities society. And Stone and Anna were probably working too, trying to find the three Lightbringers and the Teacher, and cloak them in protection.

There was a lick of fire along his arm. The Bishop had scored one.

Dante lost his patience. He drew and shot the Red Bishop at point-blank range, and then he spent a few moments on the corpse to make sure they wouldn't make a zombie out of him. Those were the worst kind of zombie Knights, ones that had indoctrinated while alive. He didn't like to use his guns. The ballistics made things tricky, and he had to retrieve his bullets.

Hanson was furiously embattled. Dante launched himself, his knives out, and started to work on the Seekers. His arm throbbed. Was the blade that had struck him poisoned? Maybe. It wasn't past them to do that, the bastards.

Dante fought.

# Thirty-Three

The stillness descended on Theo. The pain had lasted forever, excruciating incredible agony as the spell forced its way through her. It was as if something too monstrously big to ever be born was pushing against her brain, trying to find a way through, tearing a way when it could not find one.

Then…the quiet.

Theo opened her eyes.

Everyone else seemed frozen. A tear was on Mari's cheek. Elise's head was thrown back, her garnet necklace suspended in the act of breaking, the garnets hanging in the air. The bottle on the table had shattered, slivers of glass hanging suspended above the table, droplets of rum streaming towards the silver tornado of light hanging in the middle of the table. It looked like a freeze-frame of a movie, the candles caught in mid-flame, everything clear and sharp as it never was at any other time.

*Is it me?* Theo thought. *Am I the one they've chosen? White sand beaches…suntan…*

She thought about it. There seemed to be plenty of time to think about everything, and yet, paradoxically, no time at all. *Quickly, quickly, quickly.*

"I'm ready," Theo said. "I really am. If I have to die…I'm ready."

The silence lasted for a few more timeless moments, and then…

It *snapped.*

Elise's necklace broke, the garnets spilling onto the floor and the table, the little sounds of them hitting the wood and cloth and concrete suddenly ringing as loud as gongs. The bottle shattered, slivers of glass miraculously missing the women, but flying so quickly that they were buried in the brick walls with little popping sounds. A fine mist of rum sprayed outwards, igniting in a flash of blue flame. Mari let out a hoarse, barking sob.

Suzanne...

Suzanne held up her arms, as if receiving a lover. Her face was old and set and determined.

The silver tornado of power enfolded her.

*"Suzanne!"* Theo screamed, and would have tried to reach for her, but her body wouldn't obey her. She was frozen in place, stopped, in stasis, still. She strained every muscle, and still...Could. Not. Move.

The silver radiance filled the older woman, freed her long hair so that it streamed behind her in a wind that smelled of apples. "Oh," Suzanne said, sounding surprised, and then, "Perfect love. Perf—"

And then, as soon as it had winked into being, the tornado of energy disappeared.

There was a long breathless second of silence. Theo strained to move, to think, to take a single breath, but her lungs refused to obey her. Then there was what seemed to be a thunderclap, a noise so huge that it couldn't be heard, only felt along the skin and nerve endings. Theo was thrown back against the wall, her hand torn free of Mari's. She slid to the floor, dazed, seeing stars, and felt the sound end. It shivered in the air, rolling out through city like a shockwave.

It was done.

"Suzanne!" Theo croaked, hoarsely, and felt the tears wetting her face. Tears or blood? She didn't care. "Suzanne!"

Mari and Elise, stunned, lay on the floor. Mari looked as if she was sleeping. Elise was thrashing, weakly, her head thrown back and her copper hair spilling over the concrete floor.

"Suz—" Theo started to say again, but then shock swallowed her whole. She slipped into darkness before she could finish the word.

# Thirty-Four

The building was gutted.

Dante's boots crunched on snow and broken glass. He looked over the wilderness of snow and tumbled wreckage. The air was steaming around him. The snow might freeze overnight, once the sun fell.

The Cauldron stood on the corner, and it was a separate building from the toy shop next door and the Rembrandt—a small bistro—on the other side of the toy shop. The fire hadn't touched anything else.

The snow was whirling down, briefly sticking in his hair and to the shoulders of his coat before melting. Dante eased his way through the wreckage, walking carefully.

The fire department was blaming the fire on a broken gas main. The insurance would probably pay enough to open a new shop, if Theo wanted it.

"Oh, Theo," he said. "I'm sorry."

She was still sleeping, at her house. Elise and Mari were there, too. Hanson was standing guard. The witches had all been unconscious, and carrying three of them out of a burning building, while evading police and fire crews, had been an interesting experience, especially with Hanson's broken arm and Dante's sore ribs.

The snow came down, cold little kisses against his cheeks and hair. Snow wasn't quite ordinary this time of year. Halloween was next week. It would melt before then, maybe. If not, the little kiddies would have to wear plenty of layers under their costumes.

Halloween was Samhain to the witches, the season of the dead.

Dante levered aside a roof beam, his fingers slipping on the slick, charred wood. Snow melted under his hand, and he left two steaming handprints as he moved aside the beam with its weight of snow and shattered bricks.

The door to the downstairs lay there, scored and charred.

The stairs were buried under a pile of bricks.

He had to work carefully, because a wrong move might bring the rubble down and do even more damage. He wasn't particularly worried about being trapped. He could lift or burn his way out of just about anything except solid concrete. But if the temple below was unharmed, he wanted to keep it that way. The snow was coming down quickly through the ruined roof by the time he heaved the last double handful of bricks aside. He edged down the stairs, darkness folding around him.

The boxes of stock were largely undisturbed. Dante let out a sigh of relief and turned to the space that held the temple.

Miraculously, it was all right. The floor and the foundations looked solid. He very carefully *extended* a little and tested them.

They were all right. Theo could rebuild here.

He let out a sigh and turned to the wooden Goddess. Her carved face was serene and blank, and her crystal eyes dark. Dante approached her cautiously, his boots dropping snowmelt onto the concrete floor. The hardwood laid over it—he had to step up into the temple space—was the same type of flooring used in dance studios. He recognized it and smiled, imagining the four women installing it.

The altar was lost in darkness, but Dante's eyes were the eyes of a night creature. His pupils expanded, and the dark became brighter to him. The Goddess, wreathed in black lace, watched him.

There was a yellow silk scarf knotted around her graceful neck.

Dante reached out and almost touched it. Should he leave it here for Theo to find?

"Take it with you," someone said, behind him. A female voice, silvery, but hard and sharp.

Dante whirled, his sword blurring out of its sheath. He hadn't heard anyone behind him.

The basement was empty to his dark-adapted eyes, and also to his other sense. No other living thing was in here.

The blade glinted dully. Cold iron, the best defense against the Dark, not counting silver. Dante's breath came hard and deep. It made a cloud in the darkness. His ribs ached dully, and his face hurt in the scorching cold, but he was ready.

"Don't be ridiculous." The voice was slightly amused, and familiar. "Take it with you."

The yellow witch. The Teacher.

Dante scanned the building. Nothing and nobody here behind the yellow tape barring the ruined building to passersby. His sword glimmered in the ordinary darkness.

He slowly put his sword away and turned back to the Goddess. She seemed to be looking directly at him. Power still hung in the air here, as well as Theo's smell of sandalwood, Elise's fiery scent, and the smell of tides and cinnamon that followed Mari around. Over that, more recent, was the lemon smell of the Teacher, with a hard edge of silver. Not a scent made of flesh, but not a scent made of the Dark either.

Dante reached out and touched the silk. It was cold. He unknotted it carefully. "I suppose I have your blessing, then," he said quietly to the temple's silence. There was no answer. He folded the scarf and put it in the safest pocket he had, on the inside of his torn and tattered leather coat.

He turned away from the statue. Once he stepped off the wooden floor, the smell of ashes and snow overpowered the tang of Power. He climbed the stairs carefully and emerged into the thick-falling snow.

He levered the door back over the cavernous hole that led down to the basement, and bound it with a bit of Power. He had to be careful of the limited energy he had left before he collapsed. He still hadn't slept.

Before complete exhaustion took him, he used some more of the precious little power he had left to seal the space so that no looters would get in. Not that anyone would want any of the ruined merchandise that lay under the bank of freshly fallen snow. But it was Theo's store. He wanted it kept safe for her.

When he was finished, he stood on the corner for a few moments, watching the snow come down. A winter storm had appeared out of nowhere, according to the meteorologists, but Dante knew that the spell the witches had cast had played havoc with the weather system. In terms of pure Power, it was the biggest spell Dante had ever seen performed. *And I didn't even see it,* he thought. *I was busy getting beaten up.*

He sighed, frowning, his breath making a pale cloud in the cold air. His fingers stole into his pocket and felt the yellow silk. The store was completely wrecked, but it was salvageable. He hadn't failed Theo quite as badly as he'd thought.

*What am I thinking? Of course I failed her. There aren't any degrees in failure.*

He closed his eyes, his shoulders slumping. He'd failed her. The silk was soft and icy under his fingertips, warming quickly.

*Never again,* he swore to himself. *I won't fail you again.*

# Thirty-Five

Someone was stroking her hair very gently. Theo sighed, half-waking. She was still so tired.

"Theo," Elise whispered in a hoarse voice. "Theo…"

Theo stirred. "Elise?" She heard her own voice, sleepy and blurred. She couldn't open her eyes.

"The shop," Elise said. "It's ruined, Theo. The fight destroyed it." Elise sounded like she was crying. "I'm sorry. I'm so sorry."

Elise? Crying? Elise never cried. It was a point of pride.

"It's all right." Theo's eyelids were made of lead. They refused to open. The darkness behind her eyelids was comforting, kind. "We can rebuild. I've rebuilt before."

Elise's cracked lips met Theo's forehead. There was a warmth on Theo's cheek—one drop. Two. Elise's tears. "They found Suzanne's body," Elise managed, huskily. "In her bed. Hanson told me. I don't know who did that."

"Suzanne. Protecting us. Suzanne." Theo's throat was full, and she felt tears leak out from behind her heavy eyelids. Darkness and linen sheets. Her own bed. Silk against her skin— her nightgown. Familiar, reassuring. "No."

"Hanson also said we're safer now," Elise whispered. "Theo, are you listening? It worked. They're gone."

"Gone?" Theo tried to open her eyes, tried to move. It didn't work. She was so tired, so awfully heavy and exhausted. The spell had taken so much energy.

"The Crusade." Elise's fingers were warm. She smelled like cinnamon and heat. Comforting. "They're gone. Mari's okay. She's sleeping. I'm going to go back to sleep, too, but I wanted…to see you. I'm so sorry, Theo. I'm so sorry."

"We can rebuild." Against her will Theo's eyes slowly drifted open. Elise's face was bruised, and her green eyes were dark. Tears slicked her porcelain cheeks, and she sniffed, the sound of someone who has been crying a long time. Her eyes were red-rimmed and terribly sad. "Elise—"

"I'm sorry, Theo. I know how much the Cauldron meant to you...and Mexico. My God, Theo, *Mexico*. You gave up Mexico."

Theo's throat was dry and full. "I don't tan well anyway," she croaked, and Elise laughed. It was a horrible choked sound, more of a sob than a laugh. But it was better than the crying. Elise never cried.

"Oh, Theo," Elise said. But her eyes were lighter now, more like the Elise that Theo knew. "Theo."

"Suzanne," Theo whispered. "Dante."

"He left," Elise said.

"Left?" The tears were hot now, scalding. Left. He'd left. Left her. Probably gone to find someone else. Someone who didn't whine. Someone braver. Someone who could *fight*. "Dante."

"He'll take care of you," Elise said softly. Her voice was very far away. Theo's eyes drifted closed. "He just went to check on the shop and to tie up some loose ends. That's what he said. Theo? Theo..."

But Theo was already asleep, tears trickling down to wet the pillow even as she slept. *Left me,* was her last thought, and the sound of her heart breaking was the silence of snow falling around her city. The city she had given up so much to protect.

# Thirty-Six

The fire at the Tantan was blamed on gang violence and swept under the rug by an anxious City Hall, thanks to some artfully applied pressure by Circle Lightfall. That, and a generous helping of Circle Lightfall's money. It was well spent, in Dante's opinion. There were no questions. That was the last loose end he had to take care of.

He drove carefully back to Theo's little green house through the falling snow. He didn't allow himself to think of anything other than driving. He didn't want to wreck her car as well.

The windows were brilliantly lit in the gathering dusk, and he let himself into the front door.

Elise was sitting on the stairs that led up to the second floor. Her face was bruised, her lips were cracked, and there were dark, almost black, circles under her eyes. She sat on the steps with her arms around her legs and resting her chin on her knees. She was wearing one of Theo's nightgowns, a pretty emerald green one with spaghetti straps. It didn't suit her. The color was all wrong.

Her green eyes were clear but cold.

"How are you?" Dante asked. "You should be resting."

"What about the Crusade?" she asked. "Hanson told me it was done. Is it done?"

Dante shrugged. "They left in a hurry, if any of them survived at all. I do know they can't cross the city limits. They've tried." He leaned against Theo's front door, smelling the dust and sweet incense in the air. "Neither can Circle Lightfall. Anna and Stone left yesterday, after helping to deal with City Hall. It was...uncomfortable for them to stay."

Elise nodded. "Good," she said, with a ghost of a smile. Then she frowned at Dante. "What are *you* still doing here?"

"I belong to Theo," he said. "If she...if she tells me to go, I will."

Elise shrugged. "She won't." Her fiery hair seemed duller

now. "Theo's a softie. She would never turn someone away if she thought they needed help." Her eyes were hot and laser-direct now, seeming to burn a hole in Dante's face. "I'll tell you this once," she said, tonelessly. "Theo is the most beautiful soul I've ever met, and the most trusting. She's been hurt a lot. If you hurt her—dump her like her last boyfriend did, or ever raise your hand to her, or *anything*—I swear I'll kill you."

Dante believed her. At least, he believed that she would try. She might be a witch, but she was also more powerful than she should be. A fire-hair with a fiery temper. Too much power—and the responsibility of a Guardian now. Gods help them all. "I don't ever want to hurt her," he said. "I want to help her in any way that I can."

"You could start by leaving her alone," Elise snapped. "She didn't have any troubles before *you* came along. But you're not going to do that, so forget about it. She needs someone to look after her, and I can't do it all the time. So you're okay as long as you're useful. Just remember, I'll be watching."

Dante nodded. "Absolutely."

"Good," she said, and levered herself painfully to her feet. "I'm going to go back to sleep. You just remember what I've said."

"I won't forget," Dante said, and watched her make her slow way into the living room. She needed a Watcher.

*It's not my problem,* he thought, and felt a great relief at the thought. *Theo is my problem.*

He stood there for a moment and heard Hanson coming down the stairs. The blond Watcher looked haggard. He wore a torn yellow T-shirt and a pair of sweatpants that were too small for him—probably from Theo's small collection of male clothing. Dante didn't want to know why she had any in her house. "Honor, brother," Hanson said.

"Duty," Dante replied. "You look as tired as I feel."

"God, I hope not," Hanson said fervently, and Dante's mouth twitched into a smile. "They're both okay. Still sleeping. I've got to shut down for a while."

"I'll take the first watch," Dante said.

"You sure?" Hanson asked. "You know, I don't think

anything's going to attack this house. Not now."

"I guess not." Hanson was right. Two exhausted Watchers and three Guardians in a well-shielded house were more than a deterrent to any stray bit of the Dark. Later, when it became apparent that the Crusade was gone, there would be an influx of solitary predators testing the waters. That would be interesting.

Dante rubbed at his bruised and aching face. His brain had begun to turn to an exhausted mush. His ribs ached. He would need sleep to fully repair all the damage. "I'm not thinking right. Okay, we'll sleep. If anything kills us, I'll haunt you."

His attempt at a joke failed miserably. Hanson didn't bother replying, just turned around and headed back upstairs.

Dante checked all the windows and doors, just to make sure. Elise was already heavily asleep on the couch, curled up on her side. He tiptoed around her and then eased himself up the stairs.

He knew which room was Theo's. The one with the ficus tree in the window and the pale green down comforter, the stacks of books and the green and white silk kimono hung on the wall, a print of "Starry Night" on another wall, and her beautiful clothes strewn everywhere. He'd undressed her, slipped the green nightgown over her head, and tucked her safely into bed. *A perfect gentleman*, he thought, grimly amused. The truth was, he was just too tired to take advantage of her. He might have done something he would regret, had he not been exhausted and wounded as well.

Theo was safely in her bed, under the covers, so deeply asleep she hardly seemed to be breathing. Thorin the cat was curled against her side, purring as he looked up at Dante through slitted yellow eyes. Dante stood, watching her sleep for a long minute. Watching her chest rise and fall. Watching her eyelashes against her cheek. Watching the light play in her chestnut hair.

His long, torn, leather coat fell on the floor, and his sword on top of it. He laid his guns down on the nightstand, pushing aside a stack of books. His knives slipped under the pillow next to hers. He stripped off his jeans and his T-shirt, and pulled the covers back slowly.

He eased himself down next to her, and she sighed. When he slid his arm over her, she made a slight sound and rolled back against him. Thorin made a protesting sound but continued purring. Dante pulled her gently, so that her back was resting against his chest. He'd showered off the blood, and the cuts were mostly healed. The broken bones were gone, but the bruises and scars remained behind. He hadn't slept yet.

She was warm from sleeping, and he was cold from the snow outside. But she didn't even wake up, just curled back into him, her skin burning against his, the pleasure sparking through his nervous system like a spiked chain. It was a little less fiery now, a warm glow that he was becoming used to. She murmured in her sleep. Her cheeks were wet, and her pillow, too. Had she been crying in her sleep?

Dante buried his face in her hair and felt his heartbeat slow.

"I'm glad it wasn't you, Theo," he whispered into her hair. "You may hate me, but I'm glad it wasn't you."

There was no reply except a sigh. It sounded like his name.

Dante felt his muscles unstringing, one by one. She went back to sleep, but he could feel her heartbeat, and the long, deep, slow breathing that pushed her ribs out and drew them back in.

He closed his eyes. She was warm against him, and soft. He had nothing else to do now but watch over her. It was done.

Dante slept.

# Thirty-Seven

Theo came muzzily awake to the wrong sort of light. It had been dark—just past dark, actually—and now the light was the sort of clear crisp light that sometimes happens when fall turns into winter. Her head ached, as if she had slept for far too long, and she was stiff all over. She was wearing her green silk nightgown. How had she gotten into it?

*What happened?* She vaguely remembered Elise talking to her, telling her that the store was demolished and Dante had gone. Then she remembered crying herself to sleep. Suzanne, found in her own bed, protecting them once again. Dante gone.

But there was warmth behind her—hard warmth and someone breathing into her hair. Theo would have liked to savor it. It had been so long since she'd had anyone next to her, and it was comforting. But her bladder was protesting at the top of its…Well, she *really* had to take care of it.

She slid out of bed, out from under a heavily-muscled arm, and made it to the bathroom. When she finished, she stood at the sink and thought she'd better brush her teeth, since her mouth tasted foul. She did, studiously avoiding thinking about much of anything, and spat into the sink.

She was rinsing her toothbrush off when she looked up into the mirror and dropped the toothbrush, letting out a short, sharp sound. The toothbrush bounced in the sink and came to rest. The entire world seemed to stop spinning under her, and she staggered.

Suzanne stood behind her, bathed in sunlight, her hazel eyes glowing. She wore a yellow dress, and her face looked younger than Theo could remember it. Younger and lit from within, golden sparkles drifting in the air around her. *Theo,* her lips shaped, and Theo seemed to hear the word whispered directly into her brain. *Theo, it's all right.*

Theodora whirled, her hair flaring out in a sharp fan.

Her bathroom gleamed white and yellow and green in the light from the skylight set in the ceiling. Clean, shining…and empty.

Theo turned back to the mirror, and her heart leapt into her throat. She tasted toothpaste and apples.

Suzanne smiled. *It's all right, Theo. I'm here. I will always be here. This was meant to be. You are the Guardian of the City. Mari and Elise will help you. And of course, the Watchers will too.*

"Suzanne." Theo rubbed the toothpaste foam away from her mouth. "Suzanne, it was supposed to be me."

Now, Suzanne's eyebrows drew together in the warning look Theo remembered so well. *Always wanting to be the star, Theo. No. This was my choice. I knew I would be chosen to be the one on the other side of the Veil. Yours is the more difficult task, Theo. To be the Guardian of the city means that you will have to make harsh decisions.*

"Suzanne," Theo said. Her face looked gray in the mirror. Gray and shocked, the face of an old woman with green eyes. "Suzanne, I can't do this. I need your help."

*You always will have my help. And my love. Now, go and be happy. I will be watching over you.*

And then Suzanne faded in the mirror, becoming only a bar of sunlight. A sound filled Theo's head, of Suzanne's voice. Singing...

Theo found that she was humming along. *Bring me down to the god in the glen, bring me down to the green trees dancing. Bring me down to the Lady's mirror, bring me down to the place of the dance...* The song faded, and Theo felt the tears start under her eyes. The smell of apples lingered in the golden air.

There was a sound and then a tap on the door. "Theo?" Dante's voice. "Are you all right?"

She felt for the bathroom door, staring into the mirror, and yanked it open. Dante was there, tall and dark, his hair falling forward across his forehead, his face terribly bruised. There were fresh scars crisscrossing his torso, over the smoothly defined muscle. He was wearing only a pair of jeans and had a black knife in his hand. When he saw her, his eyes flicked over the bathroom, and then the knife disappeared. "Theo?"

he asked gently, as if uncertain.

"Suzanne," she whispered.

He reached out and touched her shoulders. His skin was warm and rough against hers. "I'm sorry, Theo. I'm so sorry."

She went gratefully into his arms. He hadn't left her. He held her for a long time, his skin warm against hers, until the shaking stopped and the little hurt sounds she was making evened out. He kissed her forehead and cheeks, and then he led her back to the bed and pulled the covers back.

Theo let him, but then she stopped and shook her head. "No."

Dante froze. He looked at her, his face so bruised and torn that she couldn't decipher his expression. Only his black eyes spoke, and she didn't know how to interpret what they were saying. He simply stood there, holding his breath, staring at her.

Watching her.

"No," she said. "Only if you come with me. I don't want to be alone. Please."

He nodded and gently pushed her down on the bed. Then he followed, pulling the covers up over both of them and taking her in his arms. "Shhh," he said. "Just rest. I'll help you, Theo, any way I can. I promise."

She laid her head against his shoulder. "Suzanne t-t-told me…"

"You're the Guardian of the City now," he replied, stroking her cheek.

"Does that mean you can't date me?" she heard herself ask. Her runaway mouth, as usual. The Cauldron was destroyed. Suzanne was gone.

Well, she could always build another shop. She was good at rebuilding. She'd had to do it so many times. And Suzanne wasn't really gone, was she?

Was she? Had she imagined it?

"Of course not." He sounded amused, but she couldn't see his face. She had her eyes closed. It was soothing to be held, soothing to feel Dante running his fingers through her hair. "I'm yours, Theo. If you want me."

"What about Circle Lightfall?" she asked.

"I don't belong to them," he said. "Not since the first time I laid eyes on you. They'll want to negotiate with you for Watchers to come. And Lightbringers."

"Tomorrow," Theo said, her eyes heavy. "I'll figure it all out tomorrow."

"Good call," he said. "Just sleep, Theo…"

"One thing," she said. "Are you…are we…I mean…"

"I'm yours," he repeated. "If you want me, Theo."

"Okay," she answered, and took a deep breath. Tomorrow was soon enough. She would think about it tomorrow. When she woke up, Dante would be there, and she would…

Tomorrow. Tomorrow was soon enough.

Theo fell back to sleep, smiling. The tears were drying on her cheeks.

Don't Miss
Lilith Saintcrow's

# STORM WATCHER

Coming in 2005

Printed in the United States
120097LV00003B/98/A